The MISSION

The
MISSION

A
Novel
By
Steve
Dunn
Hanson

© Copyright 1987 by Jacob Publishing
All Rights Reserved.
ISBN: 0-942241-00-2

The materials contained herein may not be
reproduced in any way nor resold without the prior
written permission of the copyright holder.

First Printing September 1987

Printed in the U.S.A.

JACOB PUBLISHING
2000 East Fourth Street, Suite 300
Santa Ana, California 92705

I owe much to my special friends Kaye Terry Hanson and Susan Waldrip for their honest criticism and constant encouragement. My wife Joyce and my children have likewise been a great support to me with their patience and their love.

Could *The Mission* be simply to discover the name we will answer to?

October 18, 1960
Mission Home
Salt Lake City

Dear Errol,

What have I got myself into? At home it was hard enough for me to sit through two hours of stake conference, and this has been a solid week of stake conferences! I think we've heard from every general authority at least once! This whole mission home business almost seems like a prison or something. I can't go anywhere without a companion! I'm surprised they trust me to go into the bathroom by myself. Ha!

Anyway some of the talks have been pretty good, but others have been really boring! Man, it seems like they're trying to cram a whole mission into a week. We've gone through door approaches, discussions, how to mark scriptures, how to memorize scriptures and rules, rules, rules!

Did you have Dr. Felt talk to you? He was pretty funny. He told us that as "our" doctor he was telling us we couldn't eat anything we didn't like. So when we're eating dinner at someone's home and they serve something we don't like, we can tell them we can't eat it on doctor's orders! I wish I could have done that when I was a kid and Mom was making me eat her parsnips and cabbage!

I didn't quite know what to make of the temple, if you know what I mean. I mean I didn't dislike it or anything. It was just that it was so different. It wasn't at all what I expected.

My plane leaves at 8:05 tomorrow morning. Mom and Dad are up from Tempe to see me off. I guess I have a twelve hour layover in San Francisco and then on to Sydney. Somebody said we get to go by jet from San Francisco. A Boeing 707 or something like that. My Uncle Jack said going up in a plane will be the closest I'll ever get to heaven. I'll write as soon as I find out my address in Australia.

"Elder" Pete

1

P.S. This whole thing is like I'm in a dream or something. Did you feel like this? I mean it doesn't feel real or anything!

P.P.S. There's a guy in my group whose last name is Elder. He's got to go by "Elder Elder" his whole mission! What a hate! Not as bad as his dad, though, who would be the elder Elder Elder!

o——ammo——⊁

October 24, 1960
Manly, Queensland
Australia

Dear Errol,

Well, it's been five days since I left the States. Well, actually four since I lost a day when I crossed the International Date Line. Anyway the time is really going fast! We flew from San Francisco to Honolulu and then to Nandi, Fiji and then to Sydney. It took us nineteen hours on a jet; can you dig that? I was really tired of sitting by the time we got to Sydney! Nandi was really interesting, though. We only stayed there about 45 minutes, but all these guys were running around in skirts and no shirts, and there were these grass huts all around the airport where people lived. It was just like out of the movies!

In Sydney, these Elders picked us up at the airport. One of them was President Norman. He's been out 21 months and will be going home the first of the year. He's the second counselor in the mission presidency. I guess that's as high as you go. I mean, in our mission an elder can't be first counselor because one of the local brothers is always that. At least that's what Elder Anderson (one of the elders that picked me up) said. I kept looking at President Norman as he talked, and I kept thinking there was only about a year and a half between his age and mine and how he was like a grown-up or a man and I was just a kid still. I wonder if I'll be like that in two

2

years? Ha! Hardly! (I mean grown up and be like a man, not second counselor!)

They drove us to the mission home, which is across the city and over the Sydney Harbor Bridge. They drive on the left side of the road, and these drivers over here are NUTS!! The way the elder was driving and the way the "Aussies" (Australians) drive I thought we were going to get creamed, and I kept thinking the Lord wouldn't have sent me all the way to Australia to get killed on my way to the mission home!

Anyway they took me to the mission home, but the mission president wasn't there so I didn't get to meet him. President Norman said President Cook was up in Townsville. I asked him when he was going to be back. He said in six or seven days. I asked him how far Townsville was from Sydney and he said close to 1500 miles! And that's in our mission! Actually our mission is 3,000 miles wide, and we take in half of all of Australia and even the islands of New Guinea! WOW!

Anyway, after we got something to eat, they took me and another elder down to the train station and put us on a train to Brisbane. (That's about 600 miles north of Sydney.) We rode that all night sitting up, so by the time I got to my "flat" (apartment) I hadn't laid down for over 48 hours! I didn't think I was ever going to be able to sleep in a bed again!

That train was something else! It was like out of a foreign intrigue movie with compartments and leather seats and wood trim and all. The people on it all sounded like they came from a foreign movie, too. They were supposed to be talking English, but I could hardly understand a word they were saying!

My new companion met me at the train station. His name is Elder Horn. We rode another train out to our "area." It's called Manly, and it's a suburb of Brisbane. That train was filthy, and I got my white shirt all black and sooty. Oh, well, it'll wash out.

Our flat is really something else! We live on the second floor, and it's just a little bedroom with a kitchen and a bath-

3

room that are both about the size of a medium-sized closet. We do have a sun porch that we can study on that's pretty nice, though. We don't have closets at all, just this "wardrobe." There is only one bed, and it's got this itchy horsehair mattress. Not too cool! The floor is covered with linoleum that looks like it was put down when they first invented the stuff! It gives you slivers, too!

Elder Horn is "different," if you know what I mean. He's a little on the plump side, and he hasn't taken a shower since I've been here! What's worse is we have to sleep in that cool bed together. I've learned to sleep on the very edge without rolling out! But I "love him" like President Winters in the mission home in Salt Lake said to do.

Actually I can't stand him! He's a real DORK! I can tell you it'll be "strugglesville" trying to get along with him for the next four or five months! This whole thing is different than I thought it would be. Tempe seems a long, long way away, and it's almost like Mom and Dad and the kids and Arizona State were all some dream or something.

Please write back soon.

Pete

P.S. Elder Horn really got mad at me this morning. He caught me spraying room freshener on the clothes he was going to wear today. They really stunk! There's big grease spots on his pants, and the zipper is broken!

P.P.S. I hope I made the right decision! About coming, I mean.

o—ᴀᴍᴏ⟩x

November 8, 1960
Sacramento, California

Dear Pete,

It was good to hear from you, brother! Sorry it has taken a while for me to answer back, but I have been so busy I haven't even had time to sleep! I've been out just over two months now, but it seems like only a day. Pete, this is really the Lord's work! I am a missionary trainer now and have just been given a "greenie" from Little Rock, Arkansas to work with. I am blessed to have been made a trainer earlier than anyone in the history of this mission. He'll learn! I guarantee it! My last companion and I had six baptisms in that two months. Not bad, huh? Of course, they weren't "ours," they were the Lord's. But we were ready to be guided by the Lord in what we said.

I have just finished reading the Book of Mormon again. I figure by the time I'm through with my mission I will have read it at least four more times and the New Testament, the D&C and the Pearl of Great Price all through four times. They are so true!

My goal for this month is five baptisms. With the Lord's help I'm going to do it! This mission is great! It won't be long before you catch on to it, Pete. Well, I've got to get back to work. Write when you can.

Your brother in the
gospel,
Errol

o—␣␣␣␣␣␣✕

November 18, 1960
Manly, Queensland

Dear Errol,

Wow! It sounds like you are really doing well. I told Elder DORK—I mean Elder Horn—about your baptisms. He said he hasn't seen that many baptisms, and he's been out nearly twenty months. He's really trunky! Every time he sees an airplane go over he stops and points up at it and says "ME! ME!" He's about to drive me crazy. He doesn't get up until 7:30 or 8:00, and we don't get out on the doors until after 10:00. He never holds study class with me so I've been studying by myself. I've been getting up at 6:00 since that's what our mission rules say so I've had a lot of time to study. I've got a lot of catching up to do as you know.

I've never even read the Book of Mormon all the way through, but I'm almost through Mosiah. Errol, I really think it's true. I've been doing a lot of thinking lately—especially about President Norman, our second counselor, and the difference between him and me. I mean there is a whole lifetime between us, and he's only 18 months or so older! I keep thinking what have I been doing with my life! Do you know what I mean?

I want you to know I really admire you and what you have accomplished. I want to be a good missionary and hope I can just be half as effective as you are.

I've got to get old Cement Bottom out of the bed and onto his bicycle a lot earlier than he's been getting if we're going to have any success. We only have a couple of contacts. One, Sister Bloom, looks pretty good. But all of the others I think Elder Horn keeps because they have TVs!

This tracting business is pretty hard for me. At least it's hard to get started on it in the mornings. Once we get going, though, it's kind of fun. But the starting part's a hate, and I don't think I could ever be a door-to-door salesman!

It's almost Thanksgiving over in the States. I guess you'll

be having your turkey and everything. Mom and Dad and the kids are going up to Grandma's in Smithfield, Utah. It's probably snowing up there, and they'll probably have the regular turkey and home-bottled beans and mashed potatoes and pumpkin and mincemeat pies. This is the first time I haven't been with my folks for Thanksgiving. Sometimes I wonder if I did the right thing in coming. I'm sure I did, but two years seems like so long and with a DORK for a companion and all—I don't know. Sorry to complain. I appreciated your letter. Please write soon.

Pete

P.S. I bought a used bike the other day. It is like one of those English racers with the narrow seats and all. All the bikes over here are like that. It cost five pounds (about twelve dollars). It was used, and it looks like it. I've named it "The Iron Lung." I feel like a little kid riding around on it. I haven't been on a bike since I was eleven!

P.P.S. I forgot to tell you we are into summer here.

o—ɑɯɯ◯☆

December 8, 1960
Manly, Queensland

Dear Errol,

I haven't heard from you since my last letter and figured you'd either written and it got lost in the mail or you've been too busy to write. In any case I felt like writing so here goes. Things aren't exactly getting better with Elder DORK. Our supervising elder, Elder Southgate, has been coming out to our flat every morning for the last four days to go tracting with us. He gets here about 7:00 and expects us to be ready to have study class with him and his companion. Elder Horn is really ticked off! He's had to get up four days in a row at 6:00!

Fortunately for Elder Horn, Elder Southgate has told us ahead of time he is coming out.

Anyway, we have a testimony meeting and prayer together before we go out tracting. Then Elder Southgate goes with Horn, and I go with Southgate's junior companion, Elder Whiting. (He's a good head!) This morning when it was Horn's turn to bear his testimony, he looked at Elder Southgate and said, "If you come out one more time this week, I'm not going tracting with you!" Elder Whiting and I looked at each other and got the giggles. Elder Horn gave me a look that would have turned a volcano into a glacier! He hasn't spoken to me since—which isn't all bad!

Elder Southgate's kind of wierd, too. He walks around with this smile that looks like it's been glued on or something. He thinks we need to look "humble" so he doesn't wear any jewelry or anything. He doesn't even wear a tie clip! What he does is take a safety pin and pins the underneath part of the tie to the top part so you can't see the safety pin, and then he has an elastic with one end hooked to the safety pin and the other hooked to the button on his shirt so the tie stays in place! He draws more attention with that contraption than if he had a ten carat diamond stick pin!

We had a special zone conference and testimony meeting last Sunday which was pretty good. All of the elders and sisters from the Brisbane area were there—about 40 or 50 of us. They just went down the row, everybody bearing their testimony in turn. That kind of bugged me. Sometimes you just don't feel like bearing a testimony and you stand up and say words.

I am still getting a lot of studying in and, thanks to the DORK, a lot of TV. We do have one really good contact—Sister Bloom. She's a young divorced lady with a two or three-year-old son. We've met with her about three or four times now, and she seems really excited about what we are telling her. It's almost as if her whole appearance has changed. She seems brighter or shinier or something. It's been really neat going over there. There's been a great spirit—except the other day when Elder Horn wore the greasy pants with the broken zipper that I fumigated. The zipper popped open right in the middle of the lesson, and Sister Bloom had to get a safety pin so Horn could at least get himself presentable to ride home to change pants. He is something else!

Anyway, I seem to be getting a little more used to the routine—only 22 months and two weeks left. Ha!

Pete

P.S. Please write when you can. I get a letter every week from Mom, but I can't talk to her like you and me talk. By the way, she said my dad hadn't been feeling too good. His stomach has been bothering him a little. He won't go to the doctor, though. You know Dad!

o——⸙⸙⸙ ⸚

December 12, 1960
"Sacto," Cal.

Dear Pete,

I got both of your letters. Listen, Brother, it gets better! Just hang in there! This mission is so great. We had four baptisms last month and led all the missionaries in Sacramento. My greenie is doing pretty good. I think he thinks I work too hard. He hasn't seen anything yet! Your companion sounds interesting to say the least.

In one of your letters you mentioned that Arizona State and Tempe seem a life-time away. I don't have much time to think about them anymore. Besides, I'm going to the Y when I get home. Dad said he would pay my way all the way through my MBA if that's what I decided to do. He's great!

I received a letter from my mission president, President Foster, congratulating me on our four baptisms. He said I was "destined to be an influential force in the mission." That is a humbling thought.

This mission is tremendous! I can't even imagine how anybody would not love it or would think it was hard. All you have to do is work and keep the commandments and things just fall into place. I think that must be just like life. I look at my mother and father. Dad's construction company is doing great. My two sisters have both been married in the temple, and I'm on a mission. We've just never had any of the problems that some others have had, and I think it's because Mom and Dad keep the commandments and work hard.

Well, that's Errol Butler's Sermon #4—but I think I'm right! Take care, brother, and may the Lord be with you.

Errol

o——ᴀᴍᴍᴏ⁾ᴙ

December 20, 1960
Manly, Queensland

Dear Errol,

Thanks for your letter. That helped a lot. You're lucky to be able to go to the Y. I guess I'll stay at Arizona State. I think I understand what you are saying about keeping the commandments and working hard and all. I think I'm trying to do that, but this mission is the hardest thing I've ever done. Not that I'm complaining. It's just hard. I can tell you Elder DORK doesn't make it any easier. He really got mad at me the week before last. He was still in bed at 7:00 a.m. as usual. I was out on the proch studying. Then I said in a loud enough voice so Horn could hear me: "How ya doing, Elder Southgate. I didn't know you guys were coming out today!"

I've never seen the DORK move so fast! He was out of the bed and into his trousers almost in one motion! In about a minute and a half he was fully dressed and out on the porch.

He looked around and of course, there was no Elder Southgate. I could feel him glaring at me, but I just sat there pretending I was studying. I was blessed with another day of silence!

The day before yesterday we were coming home from a night time cottage meeting, and all of a sudden all of the street lights and house lights went off and all of the crickets stopped chirping and it was totally silent. There wasn't a noise anywhere. I stopped my bike and just stood there. I felt really funny. It was so quiet, and it happened so suddenly that it was almost like the end of the world was here. I got goose bumps all over when I thought about that because here I was on a mission and all and wouldn't that be the perfect time for the world to end when you were trying to live righteously and you were serving the Lord? Anyway, it made me feel humble, and I could honestly feel the priesthood in me.

Well, it's almost Christmas. It doesn't seem like it. It is so hot and muggy here. Nobody has a Christmas tree, but some of the Aussies have decorated their living rooms with construction paper chains and balloons. Every once in a while someone has a green beach brush they have put ornaments on. Sometimes I feel like I'm in another world, Errol. Like the Christmas' I spent with my family were just some sort of a wierd dream, and the only real thing is sitting in Australia with a DORK for a companion. I wish I could say I always felt like I did the other day when all the lights went out, but most of the time I don't. I really think it's true, though, and I'm sure it will work out. I hope.

I really appreciate your encouragement and admire all that you are doing. I hope we have a baptism pretty soon. Sister Bloom is doing real well. She has gone to sacrament meeting with us the last two Sundays. Elder Horn doesn't think it's time yet to ask her to be baptized, though.

Please write.

Pete

P.S. I forgot to tell you about the mozzies (mosquitoes). There are billions of them! We have this netting that goes over our bed so we can sleep at night. It's got about a two-inch hole in it, though, and every once in a while one of the little guys finds his way through it, and from that time on his buzzing keeps me awake until he lands on me or the Dork and we "get" him! Fun, huh?

o———ᴄᴍᴍᴏ⋺

December 29, 1960
Manly, Queensland

Dear Errol,

I didn't wait for your letter to write because I have some exciting news! Sister Bloom was baptized yesterday! It was tremendous! She asked us if she could be baptized! Can you handle that?! I can't believe she had to ask us to be baptized! And she asked me if I would do the baptizing! Elder Horn told her it was usually customary for the senior companion to do the baptizing, but she said she would like me to do it if I could. So I did. That's the first time I ever baptized anybody, and it was great! She was crying afterwards and grabbed me and kissed me. She was like she was on fire inside. It was great, and I can see now what you mean. This mission is so great. I'm so glad I'm here!

Your brother,
Pete

P.S. Today is January 5, 1961. I didn't mail this sooner because I've had a little "difficulty." On the 30th (December), Elder Horn and I were riding our bikes to one of our investigators. We go down this steep, paved road and at the bottom it ends into a pasture, and off to the right is a gravel road that we go on to get to our investigator's home.

12

Anyway I was coming down the hill and was going about 35 or 40 miles and hour and got near to the bottom and put on my brakes to slow down to turn onto the gravel road—except my brakes didn't work! I knew I would really get torn up if I tried to make the turn onto the gravel doing 40 miles an hour so I decided to go straight ahead into the pasture.

What I didn't see was that the pasture was a foot above the road, and I hit the dirt bank and that was the last I remember. Elder Horn said I was unconscious for about ten minutes. When I came to, I could hardly remember anything since I had gotten to Australia! He told me what day it was, and I couldn't remember the last two months! I remembered Sister Bloom, but I couldn't remember baptizing her. I remembered you and my family and our landlord and Elder Horn, but I couldn't remember most of our investigators, and I had this letter to you in my pocket ready to mail, and I pulled it out and read it and it was literally news to me! I couldn't remember writing it.

I have been real scared. My memory has gradually returned over the last few days. I've been down in bed, and my head has really been hurting and I got cut up pretty bad and I sprained my wrist quite badly, too. I keep thinking about going home and wondering whether I should go home or not. Sometimes I really want to go home, but then I think it would be quitting. I just don't know. The mission president has called several times. He hasn't mentioned me going home, but I probably could if I pressed it. Elder Horn has been pretty good, too. He's been fixing the meals and all and has even been reading the Book of Mormon to me. I guess he isn't so bad. Anyway I'll let you know what I do. I just don't know.

Pete

o—ⱥⱥⱥⱥ⤳

January 18, 1961
Seaside, Cal.

Dear Pete,

Sorry I didn't get right back to you when I heard about your accident. I was transferred to Seaside and your letter went to my old address in Sacramento. Hey, you've got to be careful! I'm glad we ride in cars in our mission! I know you're concerned about your health and all, but you've got to stick it out. I know it'll work out okay for you.

This place (Seaside) is a sandtrap! It's right by Fort Ord on the Monterey peninsula. It looks like Tempe except there's an ocean sitting next to it. My new companion must be a little like yours. He's been out almost 19 months, and he's still a junior comp.! The mission president told me he transferred me here to help him get in the spirit of missionary work before he goes home. He'll work or else!

I was blessed to have another three baptisms last month before I left Sacto, and I have two ready for baptism here in Seaside even though I've only been here two and a half weeks. It's just so automatic. All you need to do is work and keep the commandments, and everything works out great! By the way, my supervising elder in Sacto told me that the mission president really thought a lot of me, and he wouldn't be surprised if I was made a supervising elder within the next couple of months. I haven't really thought that much about it. Besides, no one in our mission has ever been made a supervising elder that early before. I'll just take what comes and do whatever I'm asked to do.

Again, I'm sorry about your accident. Hang in there, Brother!

Errol

o———auuvo⅀

January 25, 1961
Manly, Queensland

Dear Errol,

Thanks for your letter and your encouragement. Sometimes I feel like I'm on a roller coaster. Sometimes I'm really glad I'm out here, and sometimes I wish I were back home. I wish I could be as consistent in my feelings as you are. I know that this is where the Lord wants me to be, but sometimes I don't feel like I'm strong enough to do it. Do you know what I mean? It's like my inside was stretching and stretching way beyond what it's supposed to do before it breaks. That probably doesn't make much sense!

Anyway, I feel a lot better. Elder Horn and I have been out tracting this last couple of weeks, and we seem to be making some progress. We're getting along a lot better now. Maybe it was my fault before. I don't know. Anyway, I found out something about him that made me kind of change my feelings about him. For one thing, he was super with me during that week or so I was in bed. I got to know him pretty good during that time because we talked a lot about our families and what we were doing before we got out here and what we are going to do when we get back home. I think I understand now why he is always getting up so late and seems to be so concerned with his health and doesn't seem to want to exert himself too much. His dad died when he was in his early forties and so have both of his uncles! Elder Horn doesn't think he's going to live past then either, and I think he is so scared of that that he's doing what he's doing to see if that will prolong his life. And here I sit for three months making judgments! I think I'm the DORK!

By the way, I don't think I ever told you about how we live over here and how the stores are and stuff. Anyway, we don't have any hot water inside the flat. There's this little boiler that is hooked to the pipe going to the shower head, and we light a flame in it (it's gas), and it heats about a gallon of water at a time. If you just let the water trickle out of the shower, it'll keep warm until you are all washed off—if you're fast! It makes the wierdest noise—a BAROOMPH, BAROOMPH—and you think it's going to explode at anytime and you are wondering what you would do if it did explode and you are standing there in your birthday suit with a big hole blown in the wall!

One of our other "conveniences" (besides mozzies!) is a flat full of cockroaches. These babies are all over the place, and they're big (about two inches long!), and they fly! When we turn the lights on at night after coming home from a meeting, it sounds like an army running for shelter as the little dudes scurry across the floor and under the cabinets.

They don't have anything like supermarkets over here. We've got to go to one store to buy our canned goods, another to buy our fresh vegetables and another to buy our meat. It takes us almost an afternoon to shop for groceries for the week. Cool, huh?

Well, that's my travel log. It's amazing what we can get used to, though! I'm getting so I can almost understand what these "blokes" are saying, and I can actually give the right change when I buy something and don't have to hold out my hand with money in it and tell the shopkeeper to take what I owe him!

I'll tell you what I am getting a little tired of, though, and that's my supervising elder's voice. Elder Southgate's got a regular voice, and then he's got his "humble" voice. Everytime he bears his testimony or gives a discussion or prays out loud, he switches over to the "humble" voice. It's kind of hard to describe, but he talks almost in a whisper and a little higher pitch than usual, and he sticks his bottom lip under his teeth when he pauses between words. I react the same way to that voice as I do to hearing a fingernail scratch on a blackboard! Oh, well. I should have learned my lesson about criticizing. I still can't help feeling like bumping him under his chin sometimes when he's got his lip like that! Do you think I'll ever make it?

Please keep your letters up. You have no idea how much they help me. Our mail must be a little screwy. I haven't got my check from my folks this month, and I'm getting a little concerned to say the least. Don't worry, I'm not going home!

> *Your brother,*
> *Pete*

P.S. Have you ever eaten a spaghetti sandwich? That seems to be a favorite lunch around here, and it's made just like it sounds—spaghetti on bread. Yuk!

o——ᴂᴂᴂ⋗

February 5, 1961
Manly, Queensland

Dear Errol,

Can you believe it, it's going on four months! It's like the United States never was, and this is all I have ever done. I wish it was as easy for me as it has been for you. I know the gospel's true and my testimony is growing all the time, but when I think I've only been out here about a seventh of my total time . . . I don't know, I'm sorry for complaining. This week has been a "downer" if you know what I mean! First of all, I still haven't got my check from Mom. I got a letter from her, too, and she didn't say anything about the check. I went for two weeks without a letter, though, so I'm thinking the letter with the check in it was lost. It better come pretty soon! I'm totally out of money! I had to pay three pounds (about $7.00) to have my bike fixed—the one prong on the front fork of my bike was bent perpendicular to the other in my accident! I paid my share of the rent and the telephone bill, and that's all I had. Sixty-five dollars a month is all that I'm getting, and I've got that budgeted down to the penny. If I don't get my

17

check from home by the third week of the month, I'm in trouble! And I'm in trouble! Elder Horn paid for all of our groceries last week, and somebody left an envelope in our mailbox addressed to me with a five pound note in it. I don't want charity!

Then our area isn't going that well. We just don't have anybody ready to baptize. We're working and Elder Horn's been getting up pretty well on time, and we've been putting in about sixty hours a week, but nothing's happening! Two days ago we had a referral sent to us. The people lived way up on the coast about thirty miles from here, but we were the closest missionaries so we went to see them. They didn't have a telephone so we couldn't call them, but we figured the Lord must want us to see them so we set aside a day to do it. Anyway, we took the train to the end of the line, then caught a bus that took us within five miles of their house and then we walked the rest of the way. I kept thinking of those missionary stories about the general authorities when they would be inspired to go out of their way to a house, and they found some-body there who wanted to hear the gospel.

Anyway, it was a real hot day, almost a 100 degrees, and we were all sweaty and dirty by the time we got to the house. It was now about three o'clock in the afternoon. We knocked on the door, and this little old man about 90 opened the door and asked who we were. We told him, and his face got all red and he shouted, "You Brighamites! You Brighamites! You get away from here with all your polygamy ideas!" It turns out this guy was a member of the Reorganites church and he hated Mormons! He slammed the door on us, and we weren't about to even ask him for a drink! Anyway, we walked back to where we caught our bus and had to wait an hour and a half for it to come, and by the time we finally got home, it was after midnight! I slept in until 7:30 the next morning.

I just can't understand it sometimes. I don't know why we don't have more success than we do. All these stories I heard about the mission and the miraculous conversions and stuff just aren't happening here! I hear about all your baptisms and wonder what we're doing or what. Maybe we've got halatosis! But then maybe it's like the dolphins. There are a lot of them around here, and a guy was telling us about all the stories of how they pushed people who were drowning to the shore and saved them. Then he said, "Of course we don't hear much about the ones the dolphins push out to sea!" I guess returned missionaries would rather talk about their successes and they"forget" to tell you about their problems and when you're listening to them, it sounds like that's all their mission was—one success after another! Of course, from the sound of things, that's what your mission is!

I am proud of you and your success. Hopefully, we will start to see some of that, too. I really think we are trying. Of course, baptizing Sister Bloom was a tremendous thing, and I'm sure my mission will have been worth it if she is the only convert. She is really something! She is so strong and gung-ho that nothing will ever shake her!

Please write when you have some time.

Pete

P.S. You should have seen us the other day. We were going to park our bikes under this big shady Mango tree, and it was full of mosquitoes! I mean, I think every mozzie in Manly was there for a meeting or something! Elder Horn went under before I did, and he threw his bike on the ground and came running out of there screaming! The back of his white shirt was literally black from the thousands of mozzies that were on him. He ran down the street, and I ran behind him trying to swat them off. It took about five minutes before I got the swarm away from him. He said he could feel them lift him off the ground!

o——ⲙⲙⲟ🜨

February 12, 1961
Seaside, Cal.

Dear Pete,

Sounds like you are having quite a time! It's strange to think you are in the middle of summer over there. Keep at it, and I know you will have success. You might want to check up on your discussions, though. When all is said and done, it is the Spirit that converts, but I know from first-hand experience that it certainly helps to know the discussions and to present them as professionally as possible. At our last zone conference, the mission president asked me to give our fifth discussion in front of the rest of the elders and sisters. Then he said that if everyone gave the discussions like that, our mission would be baptizing three times what we are already doing. (We are the third leading baptizing mission in the world right now!)

It took my companion only about a week to shape up. I just wouldn't stand for him sleeping in and not studying. He's going to have a good last few months of his mission whether he wants to or not—at least if I am still his companion that long. There's something in the wind! My supervising elder said he couldn't tell me what was up directly because the mission president told him to keep it confidential until it happened, but he told me not to get too used to Seaside or being a "regular" missionary. I don't know what that means exactly. I hope that doesn't mean I'll be made a supervising elder! I would be satisfied to be a regular proselyting missionary my whole mission. Besides, no one has ever been made a supervising elder before he's been out eleven months, and I've been out only about six. I don't mean to imply that I would disobey or refuse a call that was made to me, of course. If that's what the Lord wants me to do, that's what I'll do.

I baptized those two people I told you we were preparing, and we've got two more scheduled for next week. If my companion continues to work hard, I'll let him baptize one of these coming up so he won't feel like his mission has been a total failure.

There really are three kinds of people in this world, Pete—people who make things happen, people who watch things happen and people who don't even know what has happened! If we *want* to make things happen, that's all we have to do, and things start to happen! It's all **PMA** (Positive Mental Attitude)! You've just got to be enthusiastic and optimistic and go out and do it. It's that simple! I know that's why I've been successful out here, and I know that's why Dad has been so successful in his business.

Keep your chin up, Brother!

Errol

P.S. Sorry you're feeling the pinch financially. Hey, if you need some money, let me know! I get thirty or forty dollars more a month than I usually need, and I could send you fifteen or twenty or whatever. Just let me know!

o——ɑɯɯɒ—ᐳᵏ

February 18, 1961
Manly, Queensland

Dear Errol,

Thanks for your letter. As usual it was really a shot in the arm. I sure appreciate you and your example! Thanks for your financial offer. You are really a friend. Mom sent me another check when she found out I didn't get the one last month, though! And then just the day before yesterday I got this letter from Mom that she had mailed the first of January with the missing check. She had sent it to Manly, Queensland, *Germany*! As you remember my brother Bob went to Germany on his mission, but he's been home three years! I guess Mom just had a lapse and put "Germany" down. Anyway, I can eat again!

21

Things are going pretty good. We have a couple of families we are teaching that look like they might be "golden," but you don't know. We'll keep trying!

We really met up with some wierd ones last week, though! This one lady we gave a first discussion to just sat there without any expression on her face at all as Elder Horn gave his part of the dicussion. Then when I started, she still didn't have any expression, but she started to burp! And she kept on doing it! She didn't say excuse me or anything, just kept burping! I didn't know what to do so I just kept giving the discussion and pretended like nothing unusual was happening. Then when I was about two-thirds through, I heard this stifled laugh and looked over at Elder Horn, and his face was all red as he was trying to keep from laughing. But he couldn't hold it any longer, and he let out a bellow that was deafening, and when he got his breath, he snorted something like a horse and bellowed again.

The lady looked at him with this real shocked look and moved back on her chair like she was trying to put some distance between him and her. But when she leaned back, the one back leg of the chair snapped! She wasn't what you would call "petite"! She fell over on her side and literally rolled across the floor like a ball! I tried to help her up, but I couldn't budge her, and Elder Horn was laughing so hard he couldn't help me. She finally got up, and we decided that maybe the Spirit wasn't there good enough to continue so we left. She was still burping! I figure she isn't "golden"!

Then we went to another lady's place, Mrs. Currin. We were trying to make conversation like we do every time we go into someone's place for the first time, and I saw this bottle with a yellowish liquid and a strange looking thing floating around in it. It was really ugly and was sitting on top of their TV set. I asked Mrs. Currin what it was, and she told me.

She had a couple of sons—Brian and Mervin. Brian's about sixteen and Mervin's thirteen. Two winters ago she asked Brian and Mervin to take a loaf of bread to their aunt's place about a mile from their house. So they both got on one bike, Brian pedaled and Mervin sat on the seat and just let his feet dangle. Mervin had bare feet (hardly any kids over here wear shoes summer or winter!), and as they were riding along, his one foot got caught in the back spokes and his big toe was cut right off! He didn't feel anything, though, because it was so cold his feet were numb. Anyway, they got to their aunt's place and ran up the stairs to the front door. (All of the houses here are built on stilts or posts and are about four or five feet above the ground.) I guess as Mervin ran up the stairs his toe heated up, and he started to feel some pain. He looked down just as his aunt opened the door, and he saw some blood oozing out of his foot. The only thing he could say was, "Me blinkin' toe is gone!" His aunt took one look and fainted dead away!

They got the aunt revived and put some wrapping on the toeless foot and then went back home along the same route they took coming to their aunt's to see if they could find his toe. They found it! Anyway, when they got home, they showed Mrs. Currin the toe! She told them to get the sick thing out of her house, but her husband refused to let her throw it away! "It's part of Mervin!" was all he would say. He washed it off and wrapped it in a cloth and went down to the store and bought some formaldehyde and put it and Mervin's toe in a bottle and stuck it on their TV! It was putrid! It looked like a yellow pickle with a toenail on it!

After that story, we decided not to give a discussion! They weren't golden either!

Well, something's going up to happen with me pretty soon. Elder Horn and I have been together four months, and he's only got a month or so before he goes home so I'll be getting a new companion or be transferred or something. I don't know whether I would be ready for a "greenie" or not. It would be enjoyable being a senior comp. though, because then we could work as much as I want to work. Elder Horn has been a lot better than when I first got here, but our work week has slacked down to fifty hours or so. Oh, well, I guess I've got to learn patience as well. One thing I'm starting to really find out—I've got a lot of growing to do, and I've got enough faults to keep me occupied without worrying about my companion's faults. It's still hard! I still wonder if I was really cut out to do this! Sorry for the complaining. I really think I'm getting the hang of this way of life, and I really do want to be a good missionary.

Thanks for your example and your encouragement!

Pete

o——ᴄᴍᴍᴏ᷍ᵡ

March 2, 1961
Watsonville, Cal.

Dear Pete,

I'm glad you finally got straightened out financially. I am really blessed not to have to worry about that kind of thing. I appreciate my parents for doing the things they need to do so we don't have to worry about money. It's as easy to make money as it is to do anything. Like my dad always says, all you've got to do is follow the rules and dont' do dumb things. I know it's the same with missionary work. I had another three baptisms before I left Seaside.

As you can see by my new address, I've been transferred. Watsonville is in from the coast a ways and produces a lot of artichokes. I have been called to be a supervising elder. It is a humbling experience, but I feel I was ready for it. I'm going to miss being a full-time proselyting missionary, but I intend to produce as many baptisms as any of the elders in my district. I have eight other missionaries that I supervise. They are going to learn how to work! My new companion has been out about as long as you have. I think we will get along pretty good—as long as he does the right things! But that's my responsibility as his senior companion and his supervising elder, to make sure he does.

When the mission president called me to this position, he said I was the best proselyting elder in the mission and that if I continued like I had in the past, I would have greater opportunities to serve than even this. That is a humbling thought. Like I've said before, I would just as soon stay a proselyting elder all my mission. But if I can help the work by serving in other positions, I am willing to do it.

Well, Brother, keep up the good work. Sounds like you've had some interesting contacts to say the least! You're right in not messing around with them. We've got to get to those people who are ready to listen to us now. We don't have any time to waste with people who can't see the truth right off the bat.

This work is so true!

Errol

o——*——⟩⊁

March 10, 1961
Manly, Queensland

Dear Errol,

Congratulations! I know you will make a great supervising elder! It's just a great experience knowing you are my best friend and have been so successful. You are a real example!

Well, I finished the Book of Mormon. There are so many things in there I don't understand, but while I've been reading it sometimes I would get this funny feeling. I'd feel all warm inside, and my mind wouldn't be thinking of anything but what I was reading, and I felt like I was walking down a road that I'd been on before and it was taking me someplace I'd been to before and hadn't been to in a long time and a place that I hadn't wanted to leave. That probably doesn't make much sense, does it? But the feelings were real, and I believe it

25

was the Holy Ghost telling me what I was reading was true.

While I'm in a serious mood, I'd like to tell you about something that happened a couple of days after I wrote my last letter to you. It was about ten at night and I had just finished writing a letter to Mom and Dad and I asked Elder Horn if it would be okay if I took the letter to the mailbox which is about 50 yards or so from our flat. Anyway, I walked down our outside stairs to the lawn. It was real dark, and the street lighting is virtually non-existent around our neighborhood. The mailbox is on the other side of an old, narrow, wooden bridge that goes across a gully where the Brisbane suburban train runs. There's a walking lane on the south side of the bridge that you go on to get to the mailbox. Then on the side of the bridge where the mailbox is, this bridge pillar sticks up about 20 feet high or so and serves as a telephone pole as well. Anyway, I was going across the lawn and was thinking about home—particularly about Dad. He is still having some stomach pains, and he still won't go to the doctor! Well, when I got to our front fence, I heard this voice that said, "Don't go over there!" I stopped right where I was and looked around to see who said it. But there wasn't anybody there! I knew I heard the voice, and I got goosebumps thinking about where it might have come from. Then I looked over across the bridge to the mailbox and as I did, I saw something move by the bridge pillar. I stared at the pillar and after a while I could see that it was a large man standing in the shadows. He had dark clothes on, and I could barely see him. I just stood there for about ten minutes and watched. The guy didn't move. He just stood there, too. Finally, I went back up in my flat and watched out the window. It was at least an hour before he finally left. I just knew that I would have been in real danger if I had gone over there.

What do you make of that? Where do you think the voice came from? I know I heard it! Elder Horn thinks it was the Holy Ghost. I think that's the only thing it could've been. I'm shaking as I'm writing this. I don't know what I ever did to deserve that kind of experience. I feel so unworthy and inadequate. I know I want to do what's right, but nothing I've ever done could possibly deserve this. I really love the Lord, Errol.

Pete

o———aımv͛ɔ̶̶r

March 31, 1961
Goulburn, NSW

Dear Errol,

I wanted to get this letter off to you so I could give you my new address. I finally got a transfer! Elder Horn and I were getting along pretty good there at the end, and I'm actually going to miss him. He's going home in just a couple of weeks. Sometimes I wish that was me! Not really, though. I've got 19 months left, and I'm going to continue to do my best. I have to admit it is a little discouraging at times not seeing anymore baptisms. I kind of wanted to be a senior companion, too, but I guess I'm not ready for it yet. My new companion, Elder Bottwell, is the senior. He's been out nearly a year now, and I'm his first "junior" comp.

He's an interesting guy. He's from Nephi, Utah and is about six feet seven! Since I'm just over five ten, we make quite the contrast! He likes to laugh a lot and has a funny/wierd sense of humor. For example, the index finger of his right hand is cut off right by the middle knuckle. He got it caught in a meat cutter or something. Anyway he puts the stub of it into his ear or nose, and it looks like his whole finger is sitting inside his ear or nose! It looks sick, but I have to laugh everytime he does it because it looks so wierd! In any case, he says he wants to work hard which is all right with me. He hasn't had many baptisms either. He's been here in Goulburn about two and a half months. He said this hasn't been a real successful area in the past, but I think we can change that.

There are only two member families here. One is a young couple with two small kids, and the other is an old couple—he is from America and she is Aussie. He apparently met her on his mission back in the 1920s, and they got married and raised their family in the States and have come back over here for retirement. I haven't met either family yet but will this next Sunday. Elder Bottwell says that the younger family is not too gung-ho. I guess they have a word of wisdom problem, but they both come out to church with their kids most of the time. The older couple is real active—if you can be real active when you are the only members in town! Anyway, I guess we hold church in a Veteran's Hall or something. Apparently the elders do everything at church. The one brother doesn't hold the priesthood yet, and the older brother doesn't like to "speak in public"! Elder Bottwell says we say the prayers, bless the sacrament, conduct the meetings and give the talks! That'll be an interesting experience! At least the older sister plays the piano, and I guess I'll get to lead since my companion doesn't know anything about music. We are the only missionaries in town, too. The closest missionaries are in Canberra (that's the capital of Australia) about 60 or 70 miles away. So we are really on our own.

We don't have a flat here; we live right in the house of our "landlady." She gave us the back bedroom, and she cooks for us. I've been here two days now, and I can tell you it's a little wierd. She's a Seventh-day Adventist, and so far we've had no meat! Just all this stuff that is made from nuts and is supposed to taste like meat. It doesn't! Elder Bottwell said she does cook a nice roast on Sunday, though. I can't wait! There are a couple of other interesting features, too—like a chain drive toilet! The "water closet" is hooked to the ceiling above the toilet and you flush it by pulling this chain. It sounds like Niagra Falls when you flush it, and the first time I pulled it I ran out of the bathroom because I thought I might be drowned! Another thing that is going to be interesting is washing our clothes. The landlady doesn't have a washing machine. What we do is boil our clothes! We just throw our clothes in this big tub out back that's sitting on a gas flame and boil them clean! Sharp, huh? The house doesn't have any heating other than the fireplace in the living room either. It isn't bad now, but I can already tell it's going to be cold in a couple of months when winter hits us! My companion hasn't been here in the winter, but he says this is one of the coldest places in Australia in the winter. That's great! Here I am up in sweltering Brisbane in the summer and in freezing Goulburn in the winter! Oh, well, I'm sure I'll survive! But it makes me think there is someone in the mission home that doesn't like me too much!

It sure is beautiful here, though. The trees and bushes are all turning their fall color, and it looks like somebody dumped red and gold and tan and brown paint all over them. By the way, in case you don't know where Goulburn is, it's a couple of hundred miles south of Sydney and inland. I had to ride about 800 miles on the train to get here. I stopped off in Sydney and spent the night at the mission home so that helped. Those trains are not comfortable, and they sway back and forth all the time, and they are not very sound proof so you can hear this constant clickety-clack. After 800 miles of that you are sore and sick of hearing that noise and sick period! Oh, well, I made it!

All in all I was ready for a transfer, and I'm ready to go! I sure hope Elder Bottwell is! Write when you have time.

Pete

P.S. I saw my first "wild" kangaroos! Coming on the train from Sydney I saw a half a dozen or more grey "Roos" bounding into the bush just like you'd see rabbits there in Arizona! That was kind of exciting! I also saw a lot of parrots flying around. Most of them are kind of small with pink heads and gray bodies.

P.P.S. I forgot to tell you about the town of Goulburn. It looks like a western town in the United States maybe 40 or 50 years ago! The cars even look that old. The stores all have these western-type fronts (I think they're called facades or something like that), and the sidewalks are all wood and are raised up off the ground, and all the stores are connected to this sidewalk. The people wear this clothing that reminds me of some of Grandpa's pictures of when he and Grandma just got married. It's like going back in time. Actually, it's kind of neat!

o—◁◦◦◦◦◦◦▷⨍

April 3, 1961
Watsonville, Cal.

Dear Pete,

That was quite an experience with the voice. Those things are pretty hard to tell. You may have subconsciously noticed something over by the mailbox and then "thought" the warning. Of course, it could have been the Holy Ghost, too, I'm sure. I guess the important thing is you didn't go over there.

I'm sure you will enjoy your transfer. It is always invigorating to get into new surroundings. Your new companion sounds a little on the light-minded side. I've got an elder like that in my district, and I've had to get after him a couple of times already. It's hard for me to understand how anyone can be out here for more than a couple of weeks and not act grown up! I've got another set of elders that don't get out of bed until 7:00 a.m. If I had my way, I'd send them home! If you can't obey a little rule like get up at 6:00, then you shouldn't be out here. We've been doing with them like your supervising elder did with you and your companion, and it looks like it's working. It better be working!

We have another set of missionaries that really keep a dump for an apartment. Every time we go over there, it looks

30

like they took everything out of their drawers and tossed it all over, and I don't think they have done their dishes since they got into the mission field! In fact, one day I told them we weren't going anywhere until they had cleaned up their apartment, including doing the dishes! they may not like me, but it's my responsibility to make sure they are doing what they are supposed to be doing!

With all of this "supervising," I'm still leading our district in baptisms—I had two in March. But I haven't had much time to keep up on my studying and scripture reading. I'll still get through the Book of Mormon a couple more times before I leave.

I'm sorry you haven't been made a senior companion yet. Do you think it's because of the lack of baptisms? Of course, that isn't necessarily your fault. When you are the junior, you've got to do a lot what the senior wants, and your area also has something to do with that, too. However, I believe that it really doesn't matter too much where you are. As long as you have PMA (Positive Mental Attitude) you can do anything! I'm trying to teach that concept to the elders in my district. There are a couple who are starting to respond, but most of them seem to be satisfied with just being your average missionary who sits around and watches things happen. I guess that's the most frustrating thing in the world to me is to see people continue to do dumb things after you tell them not to!

Oh, well, that's what makes the world go around! Keep your chin up, Brother, and keep plugging!

Errol

o———ɔ⊱

31

April 8, 1961
Goulburn, NSW

Dear Errol,

Thanks for your letter. Again, it hit the spot! I understand what you are saying about the voice I heard, but I hadn't even looked over to the mailbox when I heard it. I don't know what it was, but I know I heard something! Regarding not being made a senior yet, I'm sure a lot of my problem must be me. I just want to see the things I'm doing wrong and make the changes I need to make. I'm determined to be positive—or at least try to be more so than I have been. It is frustrating not to be senior at this time, though.

Elder Bottwell is a pretty good worker, but we can't get through a discussion without him telling jokes. I've got to admit, though, he's fun to tract with. I told you about what he does with his cut-off finger. Well, he's always doing that at the doors. Usually we get a response like, "Oh, sick!" Or sometimes he'll keep his hand in his pocket and when they reach out to shake hands, he'll quickly put his fingerless hand into their hand before they have a chance to see that there is anything wrong with his hand. Then when they feel a finger is missing, they will usually turn red or something and start to apologize. Then Elder Bottwell gets this real bashful look on his face and says, "Oh, that's all right," as he puts his hand back in his pocket.

Another thing he does is coax dogs over to him, and then he flips them on their noses with his middle finger, then laughs as they go yelping off. The day before yesterday we went to this door and a middle-aged lady answered, and she looked at me and then way up at him and said, "Well, there's the long and the short of it!" Elder Bottwell didn't say a word. He just looked down at her for a couple of seconds and then thumped her on her head with his middle finger just like he does with the dogs! She was so startled she couldn't say anything for at least ten seconds, and then she broke out laughing—thank goodness! I could just see us going to jail for assault and battery!

I will have to admit, he gets in more doors than we ever dreamed of doing in Manly! Last week, we went up on this lady's porch and she had some throw pillows sitting on her porch swing. Elder Bottwell grabbed them up before she came to the door, then started to sell her own pillows to her! It was at least two minutes before she recognized that the pillows were hers. Then she started to laugh and let us in. We rarely get a chance to give a second discussion, though, but everybody in town seems to know us!

Well, I can feel it getting colder. I have to wear a sweater all day long now, and at night it's getting down into the fifties. I guess it can get down below zero here sometimes in the middle of winter. I can hardly wait!

By the way, my eye has been all red and aching. I guess I'll go to the doctor's in the next couple of days if it doesn't clear up.

Thanks again for your letters and your example.

Pete

P.S. Mom said that Dad finally agreed to go to the doctor on his stomach. I hope it isn't anything serious like ulcers or something. Dad can't afford to stay off work very long!

o—axmxo ϰ

April 23, 1961
Goulburn, NSW

Dear Errol,

Well, guess what! I went to the doctor's on my eye, and he says I've got something called eyeritis. What that means is I have to take this medicine that makes me groggy, and I have to wear a patch over my eye. That's cool having to explain at every door what my problem is! Sometimes I just don't know what's going on or what I'm supposed to be doing or even whether I'm supposed to be out here or not. I've been out six months now and have only seen one person come into the Church, and I don't even seem to be ready to be a senior companion. What's more we don't even have one person who's even close to considering baptism. We've got one lady who we are scheduled to teach the third discussion to, but I think she's going to chuck us.

Now with this stupid eye bit, I can't even read without getting a headache after five or ten minutes and the doctor says I'm not going to be over it for at least four to six weeks! And then my landlady and her diet! She's a nice lady, but I'm so sick of nut-meats and stuff—I had no idea you could make so many foods out of nuts! I can't even get close to peanut-butter anymore without my stomach starting to churn! And then there's Dad. He went to the doctor's finally, and the doctor doesn't really know what's wrong. He says it may just be a nervous stomach—whatever that means. Anyway, I guess they're putting him on a special diet to see if that takes care of it. Dad doesn't say much about it, but I know Mom's concerned.

To think I'm only a quarter of the way through! It's got to get better. It must! There is one bright thing—Sister Bloom. I just got a letter from her last week. Here is part of what she said:

"I shall be eternally grateful to both you and Elder Horn for teaching me the gospel. I wouldn't want to live if I thought that I couldn't always have a strong testimony of the gospel and always be active in the Church. It is the most wonderful thing that has ever happened to me."

She has just been made the second counselor in the ward Primary presidency, too! That's a real thrill. She is so strong!

Well, sorry to complain. I think this medication is doing

more than make me groggy! My ears feel like they do when we drive up to Flagstaff—they're popping and echoing all the time, and I'm just depressed as I'm sure you can tell. Oh, well, tomorrow is another day—and I'll make it!

Pete

o——cmmo——x

May 3, 1961
Goulburn, NSW

Dear Errol,

It's been awhile since I heard from you. I'm thinking maybe you were transferred, and you didn't get my last letters. I'll send this to your Watsonville address anyway and hope you get it. I'm sorry for being so negative in my last letter—I'm sure it was that medicine. I'm off it now, and I don't have to wear the patch anymore. I do have to wear sunglasses most of the time, though. Talk about "going Hollywood"! But it's a whale of a lot better than that Captain Hook patch! The Lord doesn't think I've quite had enough. Now it's my feet! You know how flat my feet are. Well, I bought these Aussie shoes a couple of months ago, and I don't know whether they don't have arch supports or what, but anyway the bottoms of my feet and my Achilles tendon are so sore I can't walk! I mean I really can't walk!

It came on all of a sudden yesterday afternoon while we were out tracting, and I could barely make it home on my bike. Anyway, we got home, and there was this telegram waiting for Elder Bottwell. He is being transferred immediately to New Castle (just above Sydney) and an Elder Craig is going to be my new *senior* companion! I'm still not ready I guess! Elder Craig is supposed to be coming by train from Cairns! That's up in Queensland, way up at the tip of Australia. It must be at least 2000 miles away from here.

35

That's got to be a week on the train! Anyway, I have no idea when he's supposed to be here, and I'm supposed to go down to the train station at 11:15 a.m. every day to see if he's there. (That's what time the train from Sydney comes in.) In the meantime, I'm supposed to stay at home. I'll tell you, if I was going to have a foot problem, now is the time! At least I'll get a chance to let them recooperate a little. I don't know what I'm going to do about church Sunday though. Neither one of the members has a telephone. I just hope Elder Craig's here by then!

I want to tell you about something that happened to me just after I sent you my last letter. I haven't told this to my companion or to my folks or anybody, but I know you'll understand. I'd ask that you don't tell anybody, though. It happened in the middle of the night. I was awake, and I was thinking about everything that seemed to be going wrong—my eye problem, my feet, my bike accident, no baptisms, not being made a senior comp. yet, Dad's stomach problems, etc., and all of a sudden everything started to go black. My eyes were open, and there was a bright moon and everything, but it all started to go black!

Then I felt something surround me, like another blanket was being wrapped around me, and it got tighter and tighter and blacker and blacker. I wanted to yell out, but I couldn't! I couldn't move my arms or legs or head or anything. I felt like I was being dragged down into a hole, and everything was closing in over me, and I was going to be destroyed! It was like my body was going to be destroyed! Like I wouldn't exist anymore at all!

Then I knew what it was. It was Satan! And I started to pray in my mind. I begged Heavenly Father to save me. I could feel my tears run down the side of my head, but I still couldn't move, and I kept begging and begging for what seemed like forever. Finally, I felt something start to lift off me, and I felt like it was lifting off and floating away and then it was gone, and I was laying there just sweating and shaking and praying. For the first time in my life I really felt like I was talking to Heavenly Father. I didn't hear a voice or anything, but I started to feel all peaceful, and I stopped shaking and I kept thinking that maybe that's what happened to Joseph Smith just before God and Christ appeared to him. I was really scared!

Errol, I want you to know that I know this Church is true! Not only that, but I know that Satan is real and that Heavenly Father is real and He answers prayers.

Love,
Pete

o—cccoo ϡ

May 13, 1961
Watsonville, Cal.

Dear Pete,

You're a good letter writer! I feel like I almost know Australia now. I just don't have time to pay attention to anything but missionary work and baptizing. My district led the entire mission last month, and I led my district. (I had six baptisms last month, and our district had seventeen.) My elders are shaping up now. I got one of the elders transferred who had trouble getting up when he was supposed to, and the new elder who took his place makes his companion get up, so we've got that problem solved.

I really haven't kept in touch with any of the people I've baptized. I figure it's my job to baptize, and the people in the wards and branches have the responsibility to fellowship. Besides, I just don't have the time to be writing letters to all those people. I hardly am even able to keep up sending one home every couple of weeks or so and one to you every month or so.

You've had some interesting experiences, I must say! This

last one would have been frightening. With the knowledge I have of the gospel, Pete, I don't think there is any way that Satan could get hold of me—I hope not anyway. It's fun to be successful, and that's what this life is all about. Oh, sure, everybody has some problems, but they really don't need to be too serious—only if we let them! It's when we let them get serious and we start dwelling on them that Satan comes around and starts to have some influence on us. But as long as we're doing the right things, the Lord is going to keep us from having anything too serious happen to us.

It'll be interesting what happens in the next month or so. We have four traveling elders (TE's) in our mission. I don't know whether you have those or not. But here they travel all over the mission and supervise the supervising elders. They work real close with the mission president and the second counselor. Anyway, two of our TE's go home in the next five or six weeks so it'll be interesting. I don't mean to imply I think I will be one. There are a lot of supervising elders who have been supervising elders longer than I have, so if that's the main criteria, then I'll just stay where I am. That would certainly be all right with me! At least here I still get to do proselyting work. If I were made a TE, I wouldn't have time to be teaching anybody, and that's what I really enjoy doing.

Keep up the good work, Pete. I can promise you it will all come together!

Errol

o—aaaaa҉ᴊᵗ

May 18, 1961
Goulburn, NSW

Dear Errol,

Thanks for your letter and thanks for the compliment—about my letter writing. I would rather be a baptizer like you!

Sometimes I feel like my mission has nearly been wasted from the standpoint of me doing things for other people. With only one baptism and having been out seven months, that's not exactly setting the world on fire! I have been blessed with some good experiences, though, and I thank the Lord for that!

Elder Craig finally got here. He's been out fifteen months. He's an interesting guy. He's a real bookworm and wants to be a nuclear physicist. He seems to have a photographic memory and knows the scriptures like no one I've ever seen. He said the last area he was in, up near Cairns (that's pronounced Cans) he and his companion had tracted it out and the mission president just left them there for two more months because they had so many people they were teaching. They ended up baptizing 18 people in two months, but they didn't have anything to do during the day so Elder Craig just studied. He spent a lot of time reading up on the Jehovah Witnesses and the Seventh Day Adventists. (He's already gotten into a "warm" discussion with our landlady!) Anyway, I think I'll learn a lot from him.

By the way, my eye is nearly back to normal, and my feet are okay. I wonder what's next? I still worry about Dad, though. This diet thing doesn't seem to be doing much for him. Mom said if they don't see some improvement pretty soon, they'll have to go in for exploratory surgery. That concerns me!

I felt really bad about not being made a senior this time. I know I shouldn't feel that way, but I thought I was ready. I've got to trust in the Lord more. I know it's probably more an ego thing than anything, but there's sure a lot of things I'd do different than what my seniors have done. Elder Craig is a good head, but he likes to bash too much. In fact, he asked our landlady where the local Seventh Day minister lives, and we went over there like we were tracting him out. Elder Craig massacred him. I felt sorry for the guy. He was probably in his seventies and wasn't too quick on the comeback. I just didn't feel right about it at all.

Well, winter seems to be upon us! During the day I wear my long johns besides my regular clothes, then a sweater, my suit coat and an overcoat. We haven't had a lot of snow, but boy is it cold! At night it's something else! I told you we don't have central heat. In fact, in our bedroom we don't have any heat at all! It's just as cold in there as it is outside. I can see my breath even! (Elder Bottwell said that wasn't unusual—that he's seen my breath when it was 75 out! Ha!) Anyway, it's cold! At night, I wear my garments, long johns, pajamas, robe and two pairs of socks. I have nine blankets piled on me and a hot water bottle at the foot of my bed. I wrap the blankets all around my head so only my nose is sticking out, and it's (my nose) nearly frozen when I wake up in the morning. Oh, well, I'll survive!

This letter is already long, but I wanted to tell you about a special thing that happened while I was waiting for Elder Craig to get here. It took him a full week, and I had to stay here at home for that week. I didn't mind that too much because of my feet. But when Sunday came, I didn't know what to do. The members don't have phones, and there was no way I could get hold of them, and I didn't want them to be disappointed about going to church and not having anybody there, so I decided to bike into town and open up the hall and have church. My feet were killing me, and I was freezing to death by the time I got there. I was a few minutes early so I tried to clean up the room a little. (There's always cigarette butts all over and beer bottles laying around.) Anyway, I got it pretty clean and prepared the sacrament table, and by that time it was time to start—but no members! I was freezing to death because there's no heat in there, not even a fireplace, and I couldn't walk to get warm because my feet hurt so bad, so I just sat there waiting and freezing.

After about twenty minutes or so I decided nobody was coming so I started to clean up the sacrament. I was feeling really sorry for myself that nobody had shown when I made the effort to set everything up with the cold and with my feet hurting so bad. Anyway, just as I started to put the sacrament away, in walked Sister Boyer. She's the older sister and is in her early seventies. She was all flushed and panting. When she got her breath, she told me that her husband wasn't feeling very well, and she didn't know how to drive their car and she didn't want to miss church so she rode her bike into town. She lives six miles out! That's why she was so late. She was afraid she was going to miss it and so had pedaled as fast as she could. She was so winded that she sat there for about ten minutes before we could do anything else. I was thinking of not holding church anyway with just the two of us there, but I kept looking at her and thinking about the six miles she rode and decided I'd better hold it.

It was fast and testimony meeting, so there weren't any talks to give or anything so I decided to hold a regular meeting just as if everybody was there. Sister Boyer played the piano and we sang "Ere You Left Your Room This Morning, Did You Think to Pray." As we sang, I started to forget about the untuned piano and the notes Sister Boyer was missing, and I started to listen to the words of the song. As we sang and as I listened, I felt that there were other people in that room singing with us! I know Sister Boyer felt the same thing because she kept looking up at me while she played. Since I was the only priesthood holder, I gave the opening prayer, and as I was praying, Errol, I had this feeling come over me like I've never had before. It was like my whole body was on fire, and it moved from the top of my head down to my feet. I don't know exactly what I said in the prayer, but I know I was talking to Heavenly Father. When I said amen, I looked over at Sister Boyer and tears were running down her cheeks. We sang our sacrament hymn, "How Great the Wisdom and the Love" (it's the only one Sister Boyer knows), and the same thing happened as it did with the opening hymn. Neither one of us could hardly sing, but we kept going until it was over. Then I blessed the bread, and then she and I took it; and then I blessed the water, and we drank it and all the time we were both weeping. I can't explain it in words, but I felt I understood what the Savior did for us, and I knew that Sister Boyer felt the same thing.

We bore our testimonies to each other, and I don't know what words we used, but it didn't matter because as we looked at each other, we each knew what the other one knew and felt. I said the closing prayer, and then we just put our arms around each other and held each other like a mother and son.

I am so weak, Errol! I feel so inadequate and so unproductive! I look at you and your successes with baptizing and all and at Elder Craig and his knowledge of the scriptures and the number of baptisms he's had, and I just feel like I'm letting the Lord down.

Love,
Pete

o———⚍———⚭✕

June 3, 1961
Albury, NSW

Dear Errol,

I MADE IT! I'm a senior! I also got transferred as you can see by my new address. Albury is southwest of Goulburn, right on the border of New South Wales and Victoria. We can't go across the border because that's in the other mission. My new companion is Elder Anderson. He's from a little town in Idaho called Firth. He's been out about four months, and I know we're going to get along good. He wants to work hard, and that is exactly what we're going to do! He said this town is nearly tracted out and they don't have any good contacts, but that's going to change! We're going tracting until we wear our feet off! There are only five members in town, and we are the only missionaries. There are two more missionaries in Wagga Wagga about 100 miles from us so we are really on our own.

We hold church in an Oddfellows Hall. It was only built a couple of years ago and is a lot cleaner than the place we met in Goulburn.

The five members are all one family—a grandmother, her daughter and her three kids. Elder Anderson said he just got a card from the branch president in Wagga Wagga that a male member of the Church had just moved from there to Albury and asked us to look him up. He said he didn't hold the priesthood and smoked, but maybe there's some potential there.

We're staying in a garage that was converted to an apartment. Our landlady is Dutch. She has two grown kids that live with her and her husband. They are really hard workers. She works, too, as a cook at a cafe here in town. They came over from Holland about ten years ago, and they've been able to build them a nice home (by Australian standards) and get along pretty good. Her name is Mrs. Vorhees. It's hard to understand her because of her accent, but she sure is nice.

In fact, you won't believe what she feeds us. In the morning when we get up, there's a plate of hot homemade bread, jam and milk sitting outside our door. Then after we shower we eat breakfast. So far, for the three or four days I've been here, we've had some kind of meat every breakfast, like steak or sausage or bacon, then a couple of eggs apiece, then bread and jam, hot cereal and milk. Then when we come home for lunch, she has a regular main meal with meat and vegetables and dessert. Then for dinner (they call their night meal "tea") we have meat, potatoes, vegetables and dessert, then when we get home from night meetings, there is a "supper" waiting by our door, of cookies, cakes and milk! I'm going to be a blimp by the time I get out of here! Oh, well, I guess I'll just have to suffer through!

One thing that is a drawback—our toilet is in a "little room" in the backyard! There not only is no sewer or cesspool, there isn't even a hole in the ground! All there is is a bucket under the seat! A couple of times a week this truck comes by and these guys come and get the full buckets and haul them away just like a garbage man! They call them "honeybucket men"! Yuk! I hope they are well paid!

This is a beautiful area of the country. It is not anywhere near as cold as Goulburn, thank goodness, and is green and lush. There are a lot of hills and flowers and farms. I still have to wear a coat during the day, but I don't need my long johns, etc. And we have a little electric heater for our room that keeps us warm! It rains a lot, too.

I know there are a lot of good people in this town, and we're going to find them! From the sound of things, Elder Anderson's last senior wasn't too hard a worker and was as much a practical joker as Elder Bottwell! In fact, Elder Anderson thinks he was transferred (to the mission home district in Sydney) because of his latest prank. Your mission is probably like ours as far as reports are concerned. Each week we've got to mail into the mission home a report on what we've done the past week, hours proselyted, Book of Mormons passed out and stuff. I guess what Elder Anderson's last companion did was make up a report a couple of weeks in advance, then mailed it to a missionary friend of his in Hawaii and had him mail the report at the appropriate time to the mission home in an envelope postmarked Honolulu, Hawaii! Then he wrote across the back of the envelope, "Having a great time, wish you were here!" I guess the mission president saw that and immediately called Albury to see if Elder Anderson's companion was still here or had gone to Hawaii! Elder Anderson said the president wasn't laughing, and his companion was transferred just two weeks after! I thought it was kind of funny myself!

Well, enough of my travel log. I am thrilled to be a senior and just hope I can do everything the Lord wants me to do. Write when you have a minute!

Pete

P.S. Mom said that Dad has to have some exploratory

surgery, and he goes in the hospital the 21st of this month. She said Dad just thinks it's a bother and that it's just a waste of time, but Mom is definitely worried. So am I! They still think it may be a bad ulcer or something. If you wouldn't mind, I would appreciate you including him in your prayers. Thanks!

o——ᴀᴀᴀᴀᴀ⫫

June 10, 1961
Oakland, Cal.

Dear Pete,

Congratulations! I'm glad you finally get to "do your own thing." Your landlady sounds like a missionary's dream! It wouldn't do me much good, though; I just don't have that much time to eat. Not now particularly. A week and a half ago I got a call to come into the mission home and bring my things. When I got there, our mission president called me into his office and released me as a supervising elder and called me as a TE (traveling elder). It was a shock! There has never been anyone called to that position earlier than thirteen months before, and I've only been out ten! I hated to leave my district (we led in baptisms last month again and I led the mission in baptisms with seven), and I particularly hate to have to miss teaching people and baptizing them, but I willingly accept any call that is given me.

We really have control of our lives and what happens to us, Pete. It's no accident that I am a TE at ten months. I worked for it! Nobody spent more hours than I did, nobody knew their discussions better than I did and nobody spoke more persuasively than I did when teaching. That's why I've had the success I've had. It's as simple as a formula. You put in the right ingredients, follow directions and the same product will come out everytime!

45

Keep up the good work, and you'll see continued success.

Your brother in the gospel,
Errol

P.S. I hope your dad is okay, and I'm praying for him.

o———ꝏ✕

June 18, 1961
Albury, NSW

Dear Errol,

Congrats on being made TE! I can't believe how wise you sound! I mean that. I'm sure you must be right in what you say, but sometimes it seems like I'm trying to do all the right things and nothing happens the way I expect it to or think it should. Right now, though, we are moving! This area has really been blessed in the last couple of weeks. Everything seems to be working out just great! We have met some mighty families on the doors and almost have more discussions set up than we can handle! I'm so excited I hardly know where to start to tell you!

First, two weeks ago we met this male member who moved here from Wagga Wagga. His name is Riley, and we had a great talk with him and told him the Lord wanted him to hold the priesthood and the Church needed him here. Well, he was smoking while we were talking to him, and he looked at his cigarette and said, "Well, if I'm going to hold the priesthood, I gotta give up these things!" He threw it on the ground and then took out his pouch of tobacco (they "roll their own" out here) and emptied it on the ground! He came out to church last Sunday, probably the first male member of the Church to attend a meeting here (other than the elders) ever!

Then a week and a half ago we went out on this referral we got from the mission home (the Lewis family). They're about

46

mid-forties or so and are Roman Catholic. We gave them the first discussion, and while I was giving my part it was like somebody else took over speaking and was using my voice! I can't describe it any other way. It was like I was just standing there watching my mouth move up and down and listening to what it was saying. It was beautiful, and I felt a burning inside like I did in Goulburn with Sister Boyer, and I could feel this spirit in the room and everybody else could, too.

Anyway, the discussion was on the apostasy and on Joseph Smith and the restoration and when I was finished, Mrs. Lewis said she had been so concerned because they had never had their five-year-old baptized in the Catholic church, and Mr. Lewis looked at her and said, "Don't worry about that, our baptism there didn't mean anything anyway!" Then just before we were ready to leave, we were going to have prayer and my companion gave them our little prayer discussion to teach them how to pray so we could get them to pray about the things we had told them, and he asked Mrs. Lewis to name two things she would like to know about the lesson we gave. She couldn't think of anything, so Elder Anderson asked, "Wouldn't you like to know if Joseph Smith was a prophet?" Then she looked at him and said, "Oh, I already know that!" I was so thankful for the Lord working through us like that, and I'm just sure they will be baptized! In fact, we had another meeting with them last week, and Mr. Lewis asked when he should start paying tithing! We set a baptism date for the first week in July.

Then finally, the day before yesterday we were tracting and this fellow answered the door and asked us to come in even before we could tell him who we were. He asked us to follow him, and he took us back into his bedroom (which was more like a library with all the books and things on the walls and floor). He had us sit on the only chairs in the room, and he sat on his bed. Then he said, "I understand you have a message for me." My companion and I looked at each other and then gave the discussion. He was very receptive but didn't say much. He just kept nodding his head like he was agreeing with everything we were saying. Then at the end, I handed him a Book of Mormon and told him we would like to come back and tell him about this book, and I bore my testimony to him about it. He took the book in both of his hands and looked at it without saying anything. Then he looked up at us and said, "Whenever I pick up a holy book, I say a prayer that I will open it to a passage that will be a message from the Lord to me." Then he closed his eyes, opened the book and put his finger on a page and then opened his eyes again and read where he was pointing. He was pointing at Second Nephi 33:10! Then he read that verse and the next one out loud:

"And now, my beloved brethren, and also Jew, and all ye ends of the earth, hearken unto these words and believe in Christ; and if ye believe not in these words believe in Christ, And if ye shall believe in Christ ye will believe in these words, for they are the words of Christ, and he hath given them unto me; and they teach all men that they should do good. And if they are not the words of Christ, judge ye—for Christ will show unto you, with power and great glory, that they are his words, at the last day; and you and I shall stand face to face before his bar; and ye shall know that I have been commanded of him to write these things, notwithstanding my weakness."

Then he said, "When can you come back and teach me?"

Errol, this gospel is so true! We had two other families too that we met this last week who really look good! I'm so thankful I am out here! As you know, this whole thing hasn't been that easy for me, but now everything seems to be coming together, and I'm so excited to be doing this work. I really love the Lord, and I really love these people. Thanks for being my friend!

Love,
Pete

P.S. Dad goes in the hospital in three days. I appreciate your prayers and concern.

o——ɑɯɯɯ⌐ᴈ

June 24, 1961
Albury, NSW

Dear Errol,

I just wanted to write another letter here to get my mind off things. I haven't heard anything from home yet about Dad's operation or what they found out. I thought maybe they'd call or something, but that's pretty expensive and besides they don't know my phone number so I'll just have to wait.

Things in our area here are going really good, though. We've got eight families we are teaching now! That's the most I've ever had at any one time since I got to Australia! It is exciting to see them respond to the gospel! The Lewis family that I told you about in my last letter is coming along great! We've had four discussions with them now, and they've both read the Book of Mormon half way through.

And that fellow I told you about with the Book of Mormon (his name's Eric)—we've given him two more discussions in the last week. What a spiritual giant he is! He will be our first branch president!

He said he used to belong to a spiritualist church, and the leader of his church was a woman and she was a "medium." I guess she communicated with "spirits." Of course, we know what spirits she was talking to anyway, he said that just

49

before she died he was talking to her and she was telling him about some of her experiences. She told him that Jesus was real because many of the spirits she had talked to told her that and then she said, "If I had my life to live over, I'd be a Mormon!" She didn't elaborate on that apparently, but he said when she said it, she had this far away look in her eyes like she was seeing something he couldn't, and he knew she said it because of what she knew! That sent chills up and down my spine! He said that was why he let us come in and was so receptive. This thing with his friend happened about the first of the year, and he wanted to talk to some Mormons ever since but didn't know where to locate them.

We just found on the doors this last week two more families that really look good. One, the Wagstaffs, have five kids, and the other, the Hinkle's, are from Germany and just immigrated a year or so ago, and he met with the missionaries over there and has read the Book of Mormon!

This work is so great! Finally things seem to be coming together! I'm starting to really feel like a missionary. (I even got my first dog bite day before yesterday. Fortunately, my arm went all the way to his back teeth, and he couldn't get leverage to really hurt me. It was an Australian sheep dog, too—BIG!) It's almost like I've always been out here and like I belong out here. I appreciate you, Errol, and your strength. You've been a big help to me!

Love,
Pete

P.S. Elder Anderson just got a transfer telegram, and I'll be getting a new greenie for a companion! I hate to see Anderson go; we had a great companionship for the short time we were together. But I'm looking forward to working with and teaching a greenie. I'm a little concerned about the responsibility, but I know I can depend on the Lord for help!

o—ɑɯɯɷ⋟

50

June 27, 1961
Albury, NSW

Dear Errol,

I just got a letter from Mom today. Dad has cancer of the stomach. He was in surgery for nearly five hours, and Mom said they thought they got it all, but he is going to be on treatment for at least six to eight months. I feel so helpless being way over here. Mom didn't sound at all sure about what was going to happen, but she told me that Dad said for me not to worry at all, that the Lord was involved here and I should just stay working hard and depending on Him and not worry about Dad. Financially, Mom said they were okay. Most of the doctor bills are covered by insurance, and Dad has some sixty days of sick leave built up. Mom's been taking the money for my mission out of my savings anyway.

I spent most of the day bawling, and sometimes I just don't know what to make of this life.

Pete

o—ᴄᴍᴍᴏ҉ᴋ

July 1, 1961
Oakland, Cal.

Dear Pete,

I was sorry to hear about your dad. I know it's hard on you, but everything will turn out all right. They've made some real medical advances in the last couple of years in treating cancer, and I'm sure your dad will be okay.

I love being a TE. Sometimes I really get frustrated with the elders I work with, though. You can't believe how lazy some are and how sloppy some are. I really lit into this one elder the other day. Hopefully, I was able to shake him enough for him to do something! In this position, I have been asked to

51

give talks in a sacrament meeting and at two firesides in the last three weeks since my call. I really enjoy doing that.

It sounds like you have some exciting prospects for baptism. I was just counting them up yesterday, and it looks like I baptized 37 people in my ten months of proselyting! If I stay a TE the rest of my mission and I don't get to baptize anybody else, I will still have baptized three times as many people as the average missionary in our mission baptizes in a full two years of teaching! Me and the Lord make a good team!

Keep up the good work, Pete, and don't worry about your dad. He's going to be okay.

Errol

o—ᴀᴍᴍᴏ◯ᴋ

July 8, 1961
Albury, NSW

Dear Errol,

I apologize for my "down" letter last time. Sometimes I wonder if I have any faith at all! Anyway, I got another letter from Mom, and she said the doctors were very encouraged about Dad's progress, and they are all real positive. Dad even wrote a note on the bottom of the letter. He's not a letter writer, and that's only the second time I've heard from him. He told me how much he loved me and how proud he was of me and told me to leave him in the Lord's hands and get on with my work.

He's great and I appreciate his spirit. Thanks for your interest and concern for him and me too, Errol. You are a great friend.

Well, I got my greenie! He's Elder Spackman from Las Vegas. Training a greenie is no piece of cake! Elder Spackman is a quick learner, but he's got a few other habits that he's going to have to overcome. For one thing, he's a "big spender."

52

I guess his folks are really wealthy (I think they own a big equipment dealership there in Vegas), and he never tires of telling me about it or showing me. He had to buy the best, most expensive bike (it cost nearly 30 pounds—about $70!) and opened up a bank account over here and put $500 in it! That's enough to keep me going for nearly half my mission! Anyway, he's a good guy and wants to work. He sure likes Vegas, though, and is constantly talking about it. He really got mad when I told him I thought the U.S., as a token of good will, should tell Russia they could use Vegas as an A-bomb test site! That would help thaw the cold war and would allow us to get rid of a useless piece of property! He didn't talk to me for a couple of hours! It almost reminded me of Elder Horn's silent treatment my first couple of months in Australia!

All of our investigators are doing well. We've still got the same ones I told you about. The Wagstaff's (the large family) have accepted real well. He has a smoking problem but has committed to cut down an "ounce" a week until he stops completely. He was smoking four ounces a day when we started with him, and he's cut down to three now. The Hinkle's—particularly him—are really good. He knows the Church is true, but his wife is a bit of a hang-up. She can't get serious for a minute and is always laughing. Brother Hinkle was giving this beautiful prayer, and she started to giggle right in the middle of it! That takes care of the spirit!

The Lewis' are just great. We re-set their baptism date for three weeks from tomorrow. We also set Eric's for the same time. He is the best potential convert I have ever seen. We were giving him the Plan of Salvation discussion last night, and when we were through, he just sat there with tears coming down his cheeks and said, "I wish to God that all men could see what I just saw!"

Not everything is roses, though. Riley, the member we were going to give the priesthood to, has really let us down. He said he had quit smoking and so we ordained him a deacon. We hadn't seen him at church for the last two Sundays so we went out to his place. He was out in the back doing some yard work—with a cigarette clenched in his teeth! I about wept! He didn't really have anything to say for himself, didn't apologize or anything. He wouldn't make a commitment to stop smoking, and he wouldn't commit to even coming out to church. Oh, well, with the men we are teaching now, we are going to have our priesthood here in Albury anyway!

You are a great example, Errol. I am proud of you and your successes. It feels good to start to have some of my own!

Love,
Pete

o—cmmo ⟩ʇ

July 21, 1961
Albury, NSW

Dear Errol,

To say the least, this has been an interesting couple of weeks! For one thing, this guy tried to run my companion and me over with his car! We were bicycling out on this country road to the area we're working in, and this guy drove his car right at us, coming from the area we were headed to. He just switched over to our lane and aimed for us going at least 50 or 60 miles an hour! Both of us tipped over into the ditch at the side of the road to keep from getting hit. It turns out it was a guy we met on the doors a couple of weeks ago that got really upset because he said we kept bothering him. That was the first time we'd been to his house, though! He must have been thinking we were JW's or something. Anyway, my greenie was about to go home after that!

He was already ticked off anyway! The day before that happened, our landlady and I played a joke on him. She makes these things called lamikins. They are about an inch and a half cubes made of sponge cake coated with chocolate frosting

54

and sprinkled with coconut. They are delicious! Anyway, Elder Spackman had never tasted them before and I told him how great they were and how sensitive our landlady was about her cooking and whether we liked what she served or not we had to eat it so we wouldn't hurt her feelings.

Anyway, she brought out this plate of lamikins and stood and watched us eat them. They were all "good" ones except one. I asked her to make a "special" one for Elder Spackman. She took a real sponge about the color of the sponge cake and cut it into the right size cube and dipped it in chocolate and coconut so it looked just the same as the others. She put it on the side of the plate so Elder Spackman would take it. He bit into that thing, and I thought his eyes would pop out! I tried not to look at him and ate my lamikin and kept telling our landlady how great it was. Then I looked over at Elder Spackman and asked him how he liked it. He was sitting there trying to tear his sponge apart with his teeth! He was turning all red and trying not to look like he was struggling and trying to look like he was enjoying it. Finally, when he got part of the sponge torn off, I burst out laughing and stopped him before he swallowed the thing! He wasn't too happy!

Then the morning of the day this guy tried to run us over, Elder Spackman was giving the first half of our first discussion and forgot what came next. He knows that discussion backwards and forwards, but it seems that everytime we are in front of an investigator he gets part way through and draws a blank! Anyway, to help him out I've told him when he goes blank just clear his throat, and I'll take over from there. So that's what he's been doing—every first discussion we have! So finally I told him that morning that I wasn't going to help him anymore, and he was just going to have to get through it himself.

Anyway, at this investigator's place, he forgot and cleared his throat. But I just kept looking up at the ceiling. He hem-hawed around and cleared his throat and looked over at me. I just looked at him and smiled and smiled at the investigator and didn't say anything. This went on for at least three minutes. Finally, the investigator got up and went into her kitchen to get Elder Spackman a drink of water because he kept clearing his throat all this time, and Elder Spackman took the occasion to stare a dagger or two at me, and I just smiled in return. Finally, he remembered what came next, and we finished. He didnt talk to me until after this guy tried to run us over, and he was so mad at that guy he forgot to be mad at me!

Well, on our way home, whether he did it intentionally or not, Elder Spackman swerved his bike toward me and in trying to miss him I turned my front wheel so it was perpendicular to the bike frame, and I and the rest of the bike did a dive over the front wheel! Fortunately, I was only going about ten or fifteen miles an hour. It was enough to tear my pants and literally kill the "Iron Lung"! The frame got bent, and the front wheel was mashed! I got a nice scrape on my "lower" regions where my pants tore, and a series of bruises. I looked up at him as I lay there on the ground and said, "Where in the hell do you think you're going?!"

He got this real concerned look—I'm sure because I swore—and said he was sorry. I thought about me laying there on the ground and about my bike dying and about a missionary swearing and the worried look on my companion's face, and it all seemed so funny I started to laugh. He looked at me like I was nuts, and then he started to laugh, too. I can imagine what the people going by thought with two guys in white shirts and ties with one of them laying on the street beside a mangled bike with a big tear in the back of his pants and both laughing!

Anyway, from then on my companion has loosened up a lot, and we've been having a great time. I semi-resurrected the "Iron Lung" by getting a new front wheel and straightening out the frame a little bit. At least it moves, and I certainly don't have to worry about anybody stealing it!

Then I had a real disappointment this last week. I got a

letter from the elders in Manly, my first area, and they said that Sister Bloom had stopped coming out to church. They didn't know what the matter was or anything because she refused to talk to them. They asked if I would write a letter to her and see if she responds to that. I can't believe it! I would have staked my life on her! I can't see how anybody who felt like she did when she was baptized and wrote me letters like she did could ever stop going to church! Her whole face and body glowed when she was baptized! I know she knows it's true! This whole thing has made me feel sick.

Fortunately we have the Lewis' and Eric scheduled for baptism this next week, or I'd really be down. The Wagstaff's and Brother Hinkle are scheduled for baptism in two and a half weeks, too. So our area's doing great. But I just feel like somebody kicked me in my stomach with this Sister Bloom thing. I just don't understand what could have happened.

Dad seems to be doing okay. He hates the treatment he's on, though and says it's worse than dying. That's Dad!

Well, I've rambled on long enough! It would be nice if this mission were just one steady "high"! That it "ain't"!

> Love,
> Pete

o——aᴍᴍᴏ ⫟

July 30, 1961
Oakland, Calif.

Dear Pete,

Handling a greenie really is a challenge, isn't it! You've got to let them know who's boss and make them work. That's the only way they'll learn! Sounds like you've had some experiences to "write home about." It's almost unbelievable all the things that seem to happen to you—the dog, the guy in the car trying to hit you and another bike accident! My mission has gone so smooth. I kind of expected to have some problems, but I really haven't had any. Maybe I'm just lucky or maybe I've been blessed because I've been trying to do what I'm supposed to do. The more I think about it the more I believe that everything is intended to go pretty smoothly in our lives. Maybe it's just that we mess things up because of the dumb things we do. Anyway, I'm sure that's a big part of it.

I love being a TE. President Batson, the 2nd C. in our mission, said I was the best TE in the mission and that he'd heard our mission president say the same thing. That was really flattering, but I can't take all the credit for that. I'm just doing what I'm supposed to be doing. I think anybody can, it's just that most of us don't! Batson is going home in October so it will be interesting what happens then.

I was sorry to hear about your convert falling away. It's hard to tell what gets into them. Of course, when you've had the experiences that we've had, I don't think there's a chance we'd ever fall, but when somebody's only been a member for a few months, anything can happen.

Keep up the good work. I'm glad to hear that your dad is getting along better.

Errol

o—⟶⟶)⋆

August 8, 1961
Albury, NSW

Dear Errol,

I've had better weeks! Both the Lewis family and Eric fell through! We had meetings scheduled with them the day before the baptism. When we went to the Lewis', they had their priest there. They wouldn't talk to us—they just sat there looking all sheepish, and the priest did all the talking. He said the Lewis' had always been Catholic, and Catholic is what they were going to stay. He was "polite" and so condescending it made me want to throw up! Finally I looked at the Lewis' and asked them if that was really the way they felt. They wouldn't look up or anything and just nodded their heads up and down. I couldn't even get mad at them I was so sick and broken. I was fighting to hold the tears back. They knew it was true, and they were so weak they couldn't even look me in the eye and couldn't even make a decision on their own. I bore my testimony to them and told them they would be judged according to their knowledge. I looked at the priest and told him his hands were as bloody as those that killed the Savior. He just smirked at us and said, "I'll take my chances."

Then we went over to Eric's. He wasn't there, but he left a note on the door. It said, "I still have some problems I've got to work out before I can be baptized. I have gone to Sydney until the middle of September. I will call you when I return."

Sometimes I just don't understand it, Errol. We work ten hours a day, seven days a week. We tract eight hours a day, six days a week. I pray and I beg. I want to be a good missionary! I want to be successful! And I have one convert to show for the nearly ten months I've been on my mission, and even she's gone inactive! We're trying to get the Church going here, and now our "priesthood holder" (Riley) and our potential branch president (Eric) are apparently down the tubes. And the Lewis' who are one of the influential families in Albury and could have done so much to help the Church have chucked us!

There is still some light. The Wagstaff's are scheduled for baptism the end of this month and so is Brother Hinkle—I don't think Sister Hinkle could go through the ceremony without giggling! We were going to baptize them next week, but Brother Hinkle's mother-in-law is here, and he didn't want to do it while she was here, and Brother Wagstaff said he needed two more weeks to completely quit smoking—he's down to only one ounce a day!

My companion is really down, and I've been trying to cheer him up, but it's hard when I feel the same as he does. I

59

keep telling him and myself, "It's all going to work out. Just have a little faith, and it'll all work out." But sometimes I think that something has got to start working out because I don't think I've got the faith to keep having things happen like they're happening and keep going!

I wish things went as smoothly for me as they seem to go for you, and I'm sure it's because of me they don't!

Pete

o——aumo⟩ɤ

August 17, 1961
Oakland, Cal.

Dear Pete,

Hey, Brother, don't get so down on yourself. Hey, you're trying, and that's one of the most important things. I didn't mean to imply that nothing negative ever happened to me. Sometimes it does. There just aren't any big, major things, and I think that's because I try to avoid doing stupid things, that's all.

I get so disgusted with some of these elders I work with here. They just don't seem to get their act together. You'd think if they came out here to be missionaries, that's what they'd do! Instead I catch these guys in bed at 7:00 in the morning, or they're only putting in fifty hours of work a week or their apartment is so messy and dirty you'd think they were renting a room in a flop house!

There is just no excuse for that kind of behavior! I wish I could threaten to send them home! That would get some results, I'm sure. But I can't, 'cause I'm not the boss. Besides, I've got to go around smiling and being positive all the time because the mission has adopted my slogan, "PMA." That's Positive Mental Attitude. We even got these bronze coins minted up that have PMA embossed on the one side and the "magic" triangle on the other. The "magic" triangle's three sides are "Work," "Attitude," and "Intelligent." We gave one to every missionary, and it's mandatory that they carry them with them. If a supervising elder or TE or 2nd C. ask a missionary for their PMA coin and they don't have it with them, they've got to pay a quarter fine.

This whole PMA thing and the coins and the fine were all my idea. The mission president really liked it when I told him about it, and he put me in charge of getting the coins all made and setting up the rules, etc. He seems to put a lot of trust in me, and sometimes when President Batson, the 2nd C., is out of town, the mission president takes me with him if he's visiting a ward or stake conference or some other place where he wants a "companion." I'm getting to know him very well. He reminds me a lot of my father. He is really a "doer."

I'd better end this "epistle" and get some work done. Keep your chin up, Brother.

Errol

o—aww>t

August 27, 1961
Albury, NSW

Dear Errol,

I appreciate your thoughts, but I'm not sure I totally agree. One thing I know—my dad doesn't have cancer because he does stupid things! He's a good, righteous man who wouldn't hurt anybody. He's served as a bishop and as a high councilor, and he's been the best father anybody could be. He's spent time with me and loved me and the other kids. It's true he doesn't make a lot of money, but maybe he doesn't want to. I don't know the answers here, and I don't know that anybody does. But I know he isn't stupid, and I know he doesn't do stupid things.

I'm sure I do! Both of the families we had lined up for baptism this week chucked us—at least for now. That leaves us with a big fat zero for prospects! We went over to the Wagstaff's. Brother Wagstaff was supposed to be totally off the cigarettes by last week. When we went over to his place three days before the baptism, he was stone drunk. He had his pouch of tobacco sitting on the table with his cigarette papers and just sat there with this silly smile on his face. His wife just shook her head and shrugged her shoulders. She wants to be baptized and wants her children to be but won't come in without her husband. Brother Wagstaff said he just needs more time. He couldn't even stand up without falling over!

Then Brother Hinkle told us that he'd have to put his baptism off for awhile, too. He's afraid it will cause problems with his wife if he goes ahead with it.

I don't know, Errol. I don't mean to get all over you about your ideas. I'm sure there must be something to them—at least as far as I'm concerned. But for the life of me I don't know what we could have done differently than what we've done. We've fasted. We've prayed. We know the discussions backwards and forwards. The Spirit has been there many times. I just don't know! Free agency must have something to do with all of this!

I don't know what else could happen. It seems like everything that could happen has. Yet it seems like there is another shoe that is waiting to drop somewhere. I don't know. Maybe I'm just not cut out to be a missionary. I sure as heck don't seem to be doing too good at it! I've been thinking a lot about home lately. It seems so long ago, yet I haven't even been out here for half my mission yet. Sometimes I almost wish I'd get deathly sick so I could get sent home—honorably. This thing is so hard for me, Errol. I'm trying so hard, and this thing is so hard for me and I just seem to be a failure at it.

I just don't know.

Pete

o——ᴄᴍᴍᴏ⊁

September 3, 1961
Albury, NSW

Dear Errol,

I got a call from my mission president today. He had just got through talking to Mom on the phone. Dad had a real bad relapse, and they took him to the hospital and opened him and found the cancer all over the place, and there's nothing they can do now but wait. He said Mom said they don't expect him to live past the end of the month. I need to talk to somebody, Errol, and you are my best friend. The mission president said I could go home, and I was to think and pray about it and then call home tomorrow and let them know what I decided.

I feel numb. I want to cry, but I just can't seem to cry. I keep thinking about all the times I was with Dad and how different it all is now and how strange I feel. It's like I'm just suspended here. Like I can't hear anything or see anything or feel anything. It's like I want to go to sleep and never wake up. It's like home never was, and this mission never was, and I never was. I'm so tired now. I just want to go to sleep. And sleep and sleep and sleep.

September 4—I slept until 9:00 this morning. My companion didn't wake me up. I'm glad he didn't. I asked him if he would go with me out to this hill just north of town. It's the same hill that Riley, our "inactive" priesthood holder lives on. It's a beautiful hill, Errol. It's all covered with these pink and yellow wildflowers (I don't know their names, I just know they're pretty). And when you're on the south side, you can look out and see Albury and the farmlands, and it's all green and lush now that it's nearly spring. It was pretty warm, too—nearly 70 degrees I think. There was this real soft breeze blowing, and I loosened my tie and left my bike up on the road and walked down the side of the hill about 50 yards and sat down on this rock, and my companion stayed up with the bikes.

I was thinking about all the things that had happened

these last eleven months—about my bike accidents, my sore feet, Sister Bloom falling away, Riley flaking out on us, all of our "Golden Contacts" falling through and Dad. I started to wonder what this whole thing was all about anyway. And what I was even doing out here and why I was even living, and then I started to think about the feeling I had when Sister Bloom was baptized and about the voice I heard in Manly warning me not to go and mail my letter and my experience with Satan and the fast and testimony meeting with Sister Boyer and the times when the Spirit just took over my mouth and spoke and the feeling I'd get as I read the Book of Mormon and all of the other feelings and experiences I'd had that makes me know that this Church is true.

Then something funny happened, Errol. It was like my body just peeled away from my spirit, and my spirit was just standing there stark naked, and I was seeing for the first time what my spirit was. I could see it was making a choice. It really had nothing to do with knowing the gospel was true. (I knew I knew that.) It was making a choice as to what kind of a being it was! I know this sounds crazy, but that's how I felt. I could see myself making a decision right then and there as to what kind of a person I really wanted to be. And I had this feeling come over me like the breeze I could feel on my face, and I could feel that I wanted to be like Jesus Christ! I wanted to be kind like Him, I wanted to be loving like Him, and I wanted to be faithful like Him. Then I felt my body come back on, and I felt so weak and insignificant and so far below Him and I put my head into my hands and cried.

It was funny. I wasn't thinking about Dad at all then, just about all of my weaknesses and how undeserving I was of the blessings I've been given. I wasn't feeling sorry for myself at all, and I kept seeing everything that had happened to me so far as some how being a blessing to me. I know that doesn't make sense, but that's how it felt. And then I just knew I was going to stay on my mission. It wasn't even like that was the main decision at all. It was like that decision was always my decision, and my main decision was to be like Jesus Christ and somehow even that decision seemed to have always been made, and I just hadn't fully known that until I saw my spirit there naked.

I know what I'm saying probably doesn't make sense, Errol, but it was real, and it happened. I feel like I am different than I was this morning and yesterday. I guess it was something like I read about—being baptized again by the Holy Ghost—where every cell in your body is cleansed and filled with this calm, peaceful feeling.

I called home and talked to Mom and I wasn't even crying. It was like everything was supposed to happen like it was happening, and I didn't feel sad or anything. Then Dad got on the phone. He really sounded weak, and I told him I loved him, and he told me he loved me. He asked me what I was going to do—whether I was going to come home or stay. Then I started to think that maybe he would feel bad if I didn't come home, and I didn't want to hurt him, but I knew the Lord wanted me to stay here and I wanted to stay here, and I didn't say anything for a minute or so. Finally, I told him that I felt the Lord wanted me to stay and if it were all right, I would stay, and I told him how much I loved him and I hoped he understood, and he started to cry and I started to cry, and finally he stopped and said, "Son, I was praying you would stay. I am so proud of you!" I couldn't say anything back, but thank you and I love you. Mom got on the phone, and I knew that would be the last time on this earth I would hear Dad's voice, and I started to cry again, but it wasn't really a sad cry as much as a happy cry. Do you know what I mean, Errol? I am so inadequate in expressing my feelings. I wish I had your speaking ability. I wish I could let everybody know what I know and feel.

You know what, Errol? I'm glad my mission has been as hard as it's been. I don't think I could ever have had the feelings I had today without the things happening to me that happened. I don't think I would have ever taken the time to look at myself and see me.

Thanks for listening to me.

Love,
Pete

o———anvoo———>

September 10, 1961
Oakland, Calif.

Dear Pete,

I am really sorry to hear about your dad. Listen, I didn't mean to imply that he was doing stupid things or anything. I'm really sorry about what's happening there with you. That's got to be hard on you I know. I got a letter from my folks the same day I got yours. They told me what was happening with your dad, and they said that the whole ward was fasting for him this last Sunday. I told the other TE's and the mission presidency about it, and we all decided that we would like to fast for him, too, so we set next Sunday as the day, and we're inviting all of the missionaries in our mission to join in with us. I just know that everything's going to be all right there. I want you to know I'm thinking about you and your dad, and you are in my prayers.

Your friend,
Errol

o———anvoo———>

September 25, 1961
Albury, NSW

Dear Errol,

Thank you for your letter. I can't tell you how much that meant to me to have you and your mission fasting! The people at home have been great, too. I must have gotten 30 or 40 letters this last couple of weeks, and my mission president has called me three times. I can't believe the love and concern of all these people! I'm sure my companion must think I'm a walking Niagra Falls. I just don't seem to be able to shut off the tears!

I have been praying for the Lord to help me take my mind off Dad—and He answered my prayers! Elder Spackman and I were out tracting the day before yesterday and my right side started to ache really bad. I ignored it at first because it's been kind of hurting for the last few days and I thought it might be a strained muscle or something. Anyway, it kept getting worse and worse and I could hardly even walk. We decided maybe I'd better go see a doctor, so we got on our bikes and headed for town to find one, and my side hurt so bad I could hardly stay on the bike, and I was sweating and felt real feverish. So instead of going into a doctor's office we rode directly to a hospital that was nearby.

I couldn't even move by this time, and Elder Spackman had to practically carry me into the emergency room there. They took one look at me and wheeled out a bed and a doctor started to do a bunch of poking in my mid-section and then hollered to the nurse to get me right up to surgery. It was appendicitis, and my appendix was only a couple of minutes from bursting!

Anyway, they took it out, and everything is all right except I'm so sore I wonder if they did anything! I'm laying in bed now. They had me get up this morning and walk around. This nurse helped me, and I thought I was going to die with each step. It was the first time on my mission that I had my arm around a girl! Ha!

It turns out this is a Seventh-day Adventist hospital. We've passed this place a hundred times on our bikes, and I didn't know it was one of theirs. They have treated me really good, and everyone has been super nice. I do have one complaint, though—the food. It was my home in Goulburn revisited! I hadn't eaten anything since the morning of my appendicitis attack, and I was starved! Today, they said I could have some solids to eat for tea (dinner). They brought this tray with all of these large dishes on them covered with chrome lids. It looked like I was going to have a real feast! I lifted off one of the lids and found a dish of Jello! Then under another one, I found a half a slice of bread. Under another one was a small bowl of "nut boullion" and under the largest one was a poached egg sitting in the middle of this big plate all by itself, except for a piece of parsley laying on it! I almost had to keep from crying. I had visioned I'd have a big steak and potatoes and beans and cherry pie. I had forgotten about this meat thing with them, and I guess they have a different idea than I do on what constitutes a "solid" meal! Oh, well, I'll survive! Besides, the way our landlady Mrs. Vorhees has been feeding us, I've gained ten pounds since I came here, and I need to lose it! At this rate, I'm sure I will have lost it all by the time I get out of here the day after tomorrow!

Our area is still about the same. Other than some of the contacts I've already told you about, we don't have anybody we are teaching. Now this thing! The doctor said I was going to have to stay off my feet for at least one week after I get out of here, and I can't do any strenuous activity (like tracting or bike riding!) for another week after that! So that puts our area behind another nearly three weeks!

It is frustrating, and it's aggravating! It's almost like the Lord is trying to see if I will keep to my decision about staying. I am, Errol! Regardless of what happens, I'm staying!

Again thanks for your letter and your support. Please thank your mission president, too. I know Dad will be thrilled to hear that. My last letter from Mom said he was getting weak fast.

Love,
Pete

o——⟨⟩

October 4, 1961
Albury, NSW

Dear Errol,

Well, it's been almost a year. I never would have guessed that all that has happened would have happened! I don't completely know whether I'm happy or sad about it all. I certainly don't have any convert baptisms to show for my efforts (especially with Sister Bloom falling away now), but somehow I feel that it has all been tremendously worthwhile, and I'm looking forward to the next twelve months.

I've been transferred again. I was told to report directly to the mission home in Sydney. I'm thinking that since I'm not supposed to go out tracting for another week or so, they want to send somebody down here who can work with Elder Spackman and keep me in the mission home until I can go out again. I leave tomorrow.

I'll miss Albury and Elder Spackman. We had a super companionship, and he's going to be a great missionary. I just feel bad that none of those great potential members would go through with their baptism. Eric (our future branch president) finally came back from Sydney. When we saw him, his whole countenance was different. He looked "dark"! We tried to set up an appointment to meet with him, but he wouldn't set one and didn't act like he wanted to talk to us. He said he would contact us. Then he sent us a letter asking us not to come back. I'm sure he is possessed of an evil spirit!

Oh, well, off to another adventure! I'll write you as soon as I know my new address.

Pete

P.S. Dad's still the same. I expect the final phone call any day.

o—ooooo—⊁

October 14, 1961
Turramurra, NSW

Dear Errol,

Well, how do you like the name of my new area? Both it and the name of our street, Ku-ring-gai, are Aborigine names. This is actually a suburb of Sydney. We're about ten or fifteen miles north of the mission home. It's beautiful here. The houses all have red tile roofs. Most of the homes are brick, but some are wood with bright paint. This whole area is just rolling hills, and the vegetation is thick and green, and beautiful large flowers are all over the place. It's almost like a paradise. There are Kookaburros all over, too. That's the Australian national bird. They're about as big as a large crow and are brown and white with a big head and large beak. They make this real loud noise like the birds you hear in the jungle movies. Something like a bird trying to imitate the braying of a donkey. In fact, their name means "jackass" in Aborigine language.

You ought to see this place I'm staying at! It's a big "gingerbread" mansion that's been turned into a boarding house for rich people! Elder Brandon, my new companion, says that a month or so ago he and his companion were tracting the area out and knocked on the door and gave a discussion to the owner, Mrs. Brighton. They had to move from where they were staying and asked her if she knew anywhere around they could get a room. Apparently she took a liking to them and told them they could stay here. They told her that they were sure they couldn't afford to live here, and she said, "Yes, you can! I'll give you a 'little' discount. How about four pounds a week apiece?" That's about $9. Elder Brandon and his companion looked at each other and said that was a great price, but they still couldn't afford it because they had to buy their food besides their rent. Then she said, "Oh, that includes all of your food!" They took it!

As it turns out we get five meals a day if we want—just

like at Mrs. Voorhees. Besides breakfast, lunch and tea (dinner), there are two tea breaks during the day where they serve cakes and cookies, etc.! We eat in this real formal dining room with cloth serviettes (they call napkins "serviettes"— napkins over here means diapers!) and real silver silverware and fine china plates, and you can specify what you want to eat! It's almost like a restaurant! It's fat city again for me! Fortunately, with my appendix deal, I lost all the weight I gained at Mrs. Voorhees and then some!

Then twice a week a maid comes in and cleans our room. We have to make our own beds, though! It's a tough life! I thought Mrs. Voorhees was as good as you could get, but this is amazing!

My companion, Elder Brandon, seems like a real good guy and likes to work. He's from Calgary in Canada and is really sharp. He's been out about four or five months. I'm still the senior.

In fact, I got a real surprise when I got to the mission home a week or so ago. They made me a supervising elder! That's one I can't figure out! It certainly couldn't have been because of my performance! One fall-away baptism in a year is not exactly setting the mission on fire! When the mission president interviewed me, he said some real nice things, and I felt like he had to be talking about somebody else. Anyway I stayed in the mission home a couple of days until I felt like I could move around pretty good, and then they sent me out here. This assignment scares the dickens out of me! I am so inadequate for that kind of a position. I'm going to do my best, though, and I know the Lord will help.

My side still hurts, but only enough to remind me that I had something taken out of it not too long ago. I guess we don't have a lot of tracting here anyway. I actually live within a ward! Apparently the members are pretty good with the referrals. Anyway, going over our contacts with Elder Brandon it looks like we've got enough to keep us busy day and night for awhile. I'm not going to mind that too much! I also don't need a bike. We ride the trains everywhere we go. That's good because I just left the Iron Lung in Albury because I didn't think it was worth paying the three pounds it would have cost to bring it to Sydney!

I am really looking forward to the next year! It's almost like I'm starting my mission all over again but with some knowledge! Does that make sense? This looks to be a great area (Elder Brandon said they have had a couple of baptisms a month since he got here as a greenie!) and it's going to be fun to work within a city for a change, rather than the small towns I've been in up until now!

Dad is still about the same. He is suffering so much, I almost wish it would all end. Mom said he has lost all of his hair because of the treatment and is just skin and bones. I don't want to think about it, and I try to keep the thoughts out. But they keep coming back, and it's hard to keep my mind totally on the work.

Write when you can.

Love,
Pete

o———ᴄᴄᴄᴄᴏ҈х

October 22, 1961
Oakland, Calif.

Dear Pete,

Boy, with you, when it rains, it pours! That appendix things is about the last straw, isn't it? Congratulations on being made a supervising elder! That's great!

I got a surprise, too. Our mission president asked me to see him three days ago and called me as the 2nd C. That is a humbling call! I know what you mean about hearing nice things said about you. It's embarrassing! I guess they had to have my name approved by a general authority just like a bishop or stake president! You know I will do my best!

Don't worry about your dad. I'm sure he will be all right. I felt good about our fasting for him, and I'm positive he's going to be okay.

Well, I've got to get back to work. With my new calling, I don't think I'm going to be able to keep up with as many letters as I've been sending in the past. I know everybody will understand. The Lord's work comes first!

Errol

o——————⟩⟩

October 30, 1961
Turramurra, NSW

Dear Errol,

I wanted to let you know—Dad passed away last night. Mom called this morning. She was really composed. A lot more than I was. I couldn't even speak. I started thinking that maybe my staying out here was a selfish decision and that maybe I needed to go back home to be with Mom. I tried to find out from her what she really wanted me to do, and she said if me coming home would bring Dad back, she'd want me getting on the first plane, but both she and Dad wanted me to finish my mission, and she was just fine and that me being out here doing what I was supposed to do gave her all the help she needed. I can't believe my mom!

You'd think that after all this time the actual announcement wouldn't have bothered me so much, but I spent the rest of the morning crying. Maybe it was because there was something so final about it, I don't know. I finally felt in control enough to call and tell the mission president. He is so great! As soon as I told him, though, I broke down again. He just waited patiently for me. I felt like a fool I was sobbing so hard. He didn't say anything until after I had a little composure,

73

then he said, "I love you, Pete." For a second I thought it was Dad. It sounded just like him and that set me off again. He asked me if I'd like to come into the mission home for the day and be with him and his wife, but I just felt like staying here in my flat. He is a fantastic man.

I guess the last thing Dad said was, "Tell Pete I love him and to work his tail off, and I'll see him in not too many years." If I didn't know that, this would be unbearable! I am going to be the best missionary I can be. I'm going to try to be just like my dad!

I'm proud of you, Errol, on your new calling. You certainly deserve it!

Love,
Pete

o—cxxxx⟩ɤ

November 8, 1961
Tempe, Arizona

Dear Elder Hewitt,

You don't know me, but I was talking to your mother after choir practice last Sunday, and she mentioned that you might like someone to write to. Anyway, my name is Becky Wingate. Actually it's Enid Rebecca Wingate, but who would want to go by "Enid"?! My family and I moved into the ward last June. Dad is teaching up at Arizona State now. (We moved here from Salt Lake where Dad taught at the University of Utah.) He is a professor in English. I'm going to Arizona State, too. This is my freshman year, and I'm majoring in English. What else! I've got three brothers and two sisters—all younger than I. We've been members of the Church all of our lives. In fact, I lived in Salt Lake for all of my life up until we moved here.

Summer here has got to be as close to Hell as there is on the earth! I don't know how you stand it! The swimming pool in our backyard helped, I must admit, but I got a good enough idea as to what the "other" place will be like to insure my righteous behavior from now on! The fall (if you can call it that) is marvelous! I don't mind at all being able to go outside in November without so much as a sweater on (at least in the daytime)! So I guess I'll stick around here for awhile. At least until next summer.

I wanted to tell you how sorry I was about your father. He was a wonderful man. Even in the short time I knew him, he made a great impression on me. He was always smiling, and even though he must have been in great pain, I never heard him complain. Your mother is the greatest, too! When we first moved here, she was over to our place with bread and a complete run-down on Tempe and the do's and don'ts of an Arizona summer.

Your mother talks about you all the time. Either you have her buffaloed, or you are the best thing that ever hit a mission! I won't form my opinions until I get to know you a little, but so far I'm taking her praises with a grain of salt!

I know you are pretty busy, but if you have a minute and want to, I would enjoy hearing from you. I promise I will respond to every letter you send—no more, no less.

> *Sincerely,*
> *Becky (Wingate)*
> 1345 East Del Rio
> Tempe, Arizona

o——ᴂᴂ⁀𝔵

> November 13, 1961
> Oakland, Calif.

Dear Pete,

I am really sorry to hear about your dad! I guess I was just sure he was going to be all right, with everybody fasting and praying. I know how I feel, so it must really be devastating for you. I've been thinking about it ever since I got your letter. I'm sure it must have been the Lord's will, but I'm not sure I understand why it had to happen. My heart goes out to you, and I admire you wanting to stay on your mission. I don't know what I would have done if it were my father.

I am enjoying being the 2nd C. I'm with my mission president most of the time. We speak at a lot of wards and attend every stake conference in our mission. I help him conduct missionary conferences, too. I don't get out visiting the elders at all anymore and of course I don't have time to do actual proselyting.

Again I'm sorry about your dad.

Errol

o———ɔɔɔɔɔ ⁊

November 18, 1961
Turramura, NSW

Dear Errol,

Thanks for your letter. This has been a rough couple of weeks. If it hadn't been for your letter and all the ones from home, I don't know what I would have done. They have all helped and I feel better. In fact, although it's kind of hard to explain, I know it was right for my dad to die now. I still have a hard time keeping from crying when I think about him, but I've got this real peaceful feeling about it, and I just know that everything is okay and this is what was supposed to happen. I know Mom feels the same way.

Guess what?! We're going to have two baptisms day after tomorrow! I'm SURE they are going to come through! These two are solid! Elder Brandon and his last companion met them in a grocery store. They are girls and both worked there. One's 22 and one's 23. I first met them two weeks ago, and we gave them the second discussion. We went through the discussion, and I asked them if they believed the Book of Mormon. (The elders had given them each one a week and a half before.) They had both read it almost all the way through, and they looked at me like I was stupid or something for asking such a ridiculous question and just nodded their heads up and down. Then they asked when the next baptism was! A couple of days later, the older one asked us how long she had to be a member in order to go on a mission! I couldn't believe it! The Spirit has been there so strong.

I just love this area. I have six elders that I supervise, I think I told you before. We've gone out and visited them all. Some of them need a little help! But I feel good about them all. They are all nice guys and seem to want to be good missionaries. One elder is from Wyoming. He walks like he just got off his horse and talks in a real drawl. He wears this tight fitting cowboy suit, and he has a paunch that doesn't give you a clear look at his silver belt buckle! He also wears cowboy boots. Elder Brandon said one time in church he went up to one of the good-looking sisters and told her she reminded him of Starfire, his horse! I guess he thought he was giving her a compliment. Elder Brandon said she has refused to talk to him since!

I got another surprise a few days ago. I got a letter from a new girl in our ward. Her name is Enid Rebecca Wingate. She apparently goes by "Becky." I kind of like Enid myself. It's different. Anyway, she's been there since the beginning of summer I guess, and she said Mom asked her to write. Good old matchmaker Mom! If this one looks like some of the other ones Mom used to tell me were cute, it's going to be a short correspondence! Trouble is, this far away there's just no telling! Anyway, I'm going to answer her letter to be polite. Actually, she sounded kind of interesting. Have your folks mentioned her? Mom may have mentioned their family when they first moved in the ward but nothing since. Oh, well, it will be interesting. Like you, though, I don't have a lot of extra time to be writing letters. I'll guarantee I'll keep it short!

What you are doing now sounds really interesting and exciting. I know how great a job you are doing. Keep it up and don't worry about me.

Love,
Pete

P.S. You are a great friend! Thanks for your encouragement!

○———◦◦◦◦◦◦◦◦✿

November 18, 1961
Turramura, NSW

Dear Becky,

Thank you for your letter. It was nice of you to write. A missionary always likes letters! By the way I quite like your first name, "Enid." Of course, there's nothing wrong with "Becky" either.

I'm glad you think so much of Dad and Mom. I like them, too. Of course, I'm a little prejudiced! My dad was a great man and a great example for me. This whole thing has been really hard, and I appreciate your thoughtfulness in writing.

I hope you are liking the ward. My best friend Errol (he's on a mission in northern California) and I grew up in that ward. I think it was the only ward in Tempe when I was a kid.

How do you like Arizona State? I guess that's where I'll go when I get off my mission. I haven't decided for sure what I'm going to major in. I went there for a year before I went on my mission and just took general requirement classes. Sometimes I think I want to take pre-law, and sometimes I think I might major in economics and teach it at the college level. I've got a lot of time to decide!

I love my mission! I haven't seen a lot of baptisms, but I've been blessed with some great experiences.

I appreciate everybody's support back home and thank you again for your nice letter.

Your brother in the
gospel,
Elder Hewitt

P.S. As you can tell in talking to Mom, she likes her family! You're right to take it all with a grain of salt—especially what she says about me!

∘────◦

November 27, 1961
Turramurra, NSW

Dear Errol,

What a week! It's the most exciting week of my mission! Maybe of my life! Both of those girls I told you about were baptized! It was great! I baptized one and Elder Brandon the other. It was mighty! And then today I got a letter from Elder Spackman in Albury and guess what? They baptized the ENTIRE Wagstaff family AND Brother Hinkle AND my landlady Mrs. Voorhees! I can't believe it! Elder Spackman said everything went just like out of a book. They held the baptism down at the river, and the branch president from Wollengong came to meet everybody. He said the members there were beside themselves! In one day they nearly TRIPLED the total membership in Albury!

That really surprised me about Mrs. Voorhees. We had never taught her a formal lesson or anything, but we had given her a Book of Mormon and *A Marvelous Work and Wonder*. Elder Spackman said she asked him about a week after I left if she could be taught the same way we taught the people we were always going out to see! It's just mighty! I'm so

79

excited I can hardly even write! I've been sitting here writing this letter and crying, and my companion thinks I'm nuts or something!

I am so thankful to be out here and so glad I decided to stay! I really love the Lord, Errol! This gospel is so true!

Love,
Pete

P.S. I forgot all about Thanksgiving this week! That's probably good. I would have been thinking about Dad all the time.

P.P.S. We've got a whole bunch of people we're teaching!

P.P.P.S. I can't believe this is happening to me! This must be what the Celestial Kingdom is like!!

o———∞∞∞⟩×

November 30, 1961
Tempe, Arizona

Dear Elder Hewitt,

Thank you for your "nice" letter. I don't mean to "complain" so early in our "friendship," but I'd like to hear a little bit more about what you are doing, what the country is like, what you are thinking, what the Church is like down there, what investigators you are working with, and so on. I've never written to a missionary before, and I've never even received a letter from a missionary before, and your mother told me what great, descriptive letters you wrote and here I get this "How are you? I am fine. How's the weather?" letter from you, and I'm thinking "This is a wonderful, descriptive letter?"

How was that for an opening paragraph? I'm not really that demanding! But seriously, I would like to have you be at least a "wee" more descriptive. I promise I won't be bored! I know how busy you must be now (your mother told me you had been called as a supervising elder—congratulations!), and I will understand if your letters are "few and far between."

As I promised, I will answer each letter you send. Period.

I am enjoying Arizona State. Truthfully, I miss not having most of my class members being LDS, but there is a very nice LDS Institute here and an excellent director. His name is Brother Harris. We have been discussing the Doctrine and Covenants in relation to Church history—where each revelation was given, who was involved, the reason for the revelation and the circumstances under which it was given. I find this whole area fascinating!

The school itself is probably on a par with the U. of U., although the professors seem to be more casual here. Maybe it's because of the warmer climate. That would be an interesting study in and of itself! I don't feel as "at home" on the campus, though. The buildings here are so new and so— brown! I like more traditional architecture, the color "white," and a little "age" to the buildings. I believe that gives them some character. To know that thousands have learned in a building for years before you almost creates an aura of learning about the facility that is thick enough to feel with your hand! I guess some of these ultra-modern designs, like the Frank Lloyd Wright "space station" creation here on campus, have a beauty of sorts about them, but they don't appeal to me. Something like a Picasso compared to a Rembrandt, I suppose.

In answer to your question, I do enjoy the ward. The members are extremely friendly, and I must say there are some nice looking young men there! I have generally been too busy with my studies to date much however.

I trust you had a good Thanksgiving—or do they even have that over there? Of course they wouldn't, would they? In any case, we had a good one. We stayed here and had my grandparents from Bountiful, Utah come down. They're my mother's folks. Dad's parents both died when I was small. It

81

felt strange to be walking outside at Thanksgiving without even a sweater on! I think it was 75 degrees out! I "sort of" miss the snow (I love to ski!), but I think I prefer 75 degree Thanksgivings!

Well, I've about worn your ears off (or should I say eyes?) with my ramblings. I really did appreciate your letter! You should know that you are in my prayers (along with ALL of the missionaries).

> *Sincerely,*
> *Becky Wingate*

P.S. I'm glad you like my first name (Enid) and find "nothing wrong" with "Becky." But if it's all right with you, I will continue to use "Becky" as my name.

o——⟋

December 4, 1961
Turramurra, NSW

Dear Errol,

I just wanted to keep you up on what's happening. We've been so busy I hardly know which way to turn! For the next two weeks, we are booked up with at least two cottage meetings each night. We've got to be careful so we have time to concentrate on those who are ready for baptism! What a great situation to be in! We have two more baptisms coming up this weekend. One of the members introduced us to this family with two teenage kids, a girl who's fifteen and a boy who is fourteen. The parents aren't interested, but they want their kids baptized in the worst way. The kids have been quite receptive but resent their parents pushing them. They both said they wanted to be baptized, although I'm sure the parents are doing something to bribe them but I don't know what it is! Isn't it interesting the parents know it's good for their kids, but they won't accept it for themselves! I've been thinking about it and have come to the conclusion that we should go ahead with the baptisms. The kids seem to want the Church and baptizing them and giving them the Holy Ghost will be the best thing we could possibly do for them.

For the most part my district is going real well. I don't take credit for that; there are just some super sharp elders here. There was one little problem, though. We went out to one of our elders' flats the other day, and it reminded me of the one you were telling me about that looked like a flop house! We got there about 7:00 a.m., and both elders were still in bed. I was about to really lay into them when I got kind of a strange feeling. As I looked around the apartment while the elders were getting dressed and shaved and stuff, I started to think that maybe these guys were really trying! I really didn't know what kind of a home they came from. Maybe they had never been taught to keep a clean room, or maybe this was clean in comparison to what they came from! I thought the same thing about them sleeping in. Maybe getting up at 7:00 (let alone 6:00) was a monumental effort for them! Maybe they had never gotten up that early in their life! My point to myself was I just didn't know! I knew we had mission rules and all, but it seemed to me that I had no right laying into them without knowing a little bit about their backgrounds and maybe not even then.

Anyway, when they were ready for the day, we all sat down (I had cleared some room by then!), and I suggested that we each take four or five minutes and tell something about ourselves—where we came from, what our parents did in the Church, where our fathers worked, etc. As it turns out, the one elder came from a little town in southeastern Idaho, and his dad worked on the railroad. There were ten kids in their family, and he was the only one who was active in the Church. He said his dad was gone out of town on work gangs all the time, and his mother didn't like to stick around the house with all those kids and would usually go over to her friend's place and leave the kids to take care of themselves. He said that the ward was supporting him on his mission and that his folks were really mad when he decided to go and that he had been out on his mission now for nearly ten months and he hadn't heard a word from either one of them!

His junior companion was from somewhere in the Los Angeles area near a place he called "Watts." I've never heard of it, but apparently it is quite a rough place. He said his folks and brother and two sisters were active in the Church and had always been but that he had dropped out when he was thirteen or fourteen and had messed around with street gangs. I guess he was a real trouble maker for a number of years. He said he had a bishop that wouldn't give up on him and that from the time he was seventeen on, the bishop called him every week! At first, I guess he thought the bishop was a real pain, but after six months or so he started to think the bishop must really like him and was genuinely concerned about him. Finally, when he turned eighteen (he hadn't graduated from high school yet, although he should have), he started to come out to church again. The bishop kept working with him, and he finished high school and accepted a mission call from his bishop. He said his dad was a milkman, and his mother worked as a waitress to make enough income to live on, but they couldn't support him on the mission and that his bishop was sending him most of his money.

I don't think either one of them had told their stories to any mission leaders before, and they both got quite emotional. We were certainly taking up a lot more than five minutes each, but getting out proselyting didn't seem to be the most important thing at the time. I can tell you that I certainly didn't feel like laying into them after they were finished!

I don't know whether what I did was the right thing to do or not or whether my TE would approve, but I felt right about it. I told them both how much I admired them and what a good job they were doing. I mentioned the mission rules about clean apartments, getting up at 6:00 a.m., etc., and asked them whether they thought they could do that or whether it was too tough for them right now. I wasn't mad or being sarcastic or anything. The senior companion looked at me and said, "What if we think it's too tough for us right now—what will you do, tell the mission president?"

I just shook my head and told him I wouldn't do that, and then I asked him to tell me what he and his companion could live with. He and his companion looked at each other, and then he said, "How about if we try 6:30 for awhile?" I asked him about the way they were keeping the apartment up. They both looked real sheepish, and he said they could do a lot better than that.

By this time, Elder Brandon and I had to leave so we wouldn't miss an appointment and we didn't even get to go out with them, but we felt really good about it. I really think they are going to try harder. I don't know what kind of a missionary I would be if I had come from the situations they came from. I've been thinking about that a lot, and I'm starting to think that this whole judging thing is all wrong. I've been wrong so many times—remember the problems I had with my first companion? Anyway, maybe how far along we are on the "gospel road" is not nearly as important as just being on the road. I don't know.

Well, I got another letter from this Becky Wingate I told you about. I had sent her a short, general kind of letter. She sounds really educated and sophisticated and kind of chewed me out for not sending a more detailed letter to her! She does sound interesting, to say the least! I wish I knew what she looks like. I think I'll write her another letter and ask her to send a picture. She did say she hadn't gone on many dates because she has "been too busy with my studies to date much"! That doesn't sound too good! Since when does studying keep a *good-looking* girl from dating very much?

We'll see what happens! This letter has gone on and on! Don't feel obligated to match it! Ha!

Love,
Pete

○——⦿⦿⦿⦿⦿—⋊

December 10, 1961
Turramurra, NSW

Dear Becky,

You are quite a letter writer! I certainly don't hope to match your skill! I'm sorry I was so general in my first letter, but . . . well, I really don't have any excuse! Also, I didn't intend to imply that I didn't like "Becky" as your name. It certainly is pretty. It's just that there is something different about "Enid" that appeals to me, that's all.

I kind of agree with how you feel about Arizona State. I like old buildings, too. In fact, all of Mom's and Dad's living-room furniture is antique. Most of it is mahogony, but they have a few dark oak pieces, too. After living around that kind of furniture, seeing all of this "Danish Modern" and blond furniture that came out a few years ago leaves me a little cold!

I am really enjoying my mission. My companion, Elder Brandon comes from Calgary, Alberta, Canada, and we get along very well. I have some great elders I work with here in my district. There are three sets besides Elder Brandon and myself, and they are scattered over the Sydney suburban area north of the harbor. We visit them and our contacts primarily by electric train. The trains are all on top of the ground and are quite economical to ride. We can go clear into the mission home in Wolstencraft, about fifteen miles away, for a shilling (about ten to twelve cents).

Sydney is a beautiful city. Of course, this is summer time here and can get very warm—although not like Tempe! It is a little distracting for the elders down in the beach areas (two of "my" elders are right on the beach) because the girls over here like to get sun tans ALL over their bodies, if you know what I mean. Anyway, as I was saying, Sydney is a beautiful city. The beaches stretch on and on with miles of snow-white sand. The great Sydney harbor is one of the most famous, and I think beautiful ones in the world. It is very deep, wide and long. The Sydney Harbor Bridge connects our side with the main city itself. It looks like some monstrous coat hanger sitting out there. We don't get into the city too much since it's really out of our area. There are some great museums in there, though, and even though there is a lot of new building going on, there are lots of old buildings that are at least a hundred or more years old. I like those!

Our ward here is really good. We meet in a brand new building, and it is beautiful. I haven't seen any in America that look like it. It's big and very modern looking. I think the Church wanted to make it a show place! They succeeded! Of course, the ward is not like the ones back home. There are only about half as many out to church here as in your ward, and there are a lot more inactives. We are trying to get the youth going and excited about missionary work. I think we are having some success.

Well, I hope I haven't bored you here, but you did ask for a travelog! I appreciate very much being included in your prayers with ALL of the other missionaries! Believe me, I can use all of the prayers you care to send! This is a great work, and I love it! Thanks again for your letter.

Sincerely,
Elder Hewitt

P.S. If you've got an extra picture laying around, I would appreciate you sending it. It's always nice to "see" who you're talking to.

∘———⊶⊶⊶⟩⋆

December 15, 1961
Turramurra, NSW

Dear Errol,

Well, it's nearly my second Christmas away from home. It feels like this is where I've always been, and this is where I belong. Tempe and the family and the ward and Bishop Hunt and everybody seem like people and places I read about in a book. They almost don't seem "real" anymore! In fact, Dad almost seems to be the only thing that's real—maybe because I've been thinking about him so much. It's a wierd feeling! Of course I hear from Mom every week, but it's like she is a "letter," almost, rather than a real person. It's wierd! Anyway, she seems to be getting along great, but I can tell she's lonely. She never complains, though—you know Mom!

This mission is so great! We baptized those two kids I told you about. I'm glad we did. They both were really happy, and their parents have even talked about coming out to church themselves! We have three more scheduled for the day after Christmas. One is a ten-year-old daughter of an inactive member, and the other two are an eighteen-year-old girl and her sixteen-year-old brother. They have been attending church for several months now, and we just finished giving them the last discussion. Their hang up was pretty well their dad. He didn't want to give his permission until he was sure they were sure. They've been "instant" Mormons (all you have to do is add water!) since they started coming out to church. In fact, the girl is in her MIA class presidency!

It's great to be baptizing! I just keep thinking about these kids we are baptizing and how much their lives are going to be changed!

I sent another letter off to this Becky Wingate. I haven't heard back yet. I asked her for her picture. If she doesn't send one, my correspondence will suddenly stop!

Merry Christmas! Write when you have a minute.

Love,
Pete

o———ᴄᴄᴄᴄᴏ ⟩ᴛ

December 18, 1961
Tempe, Arizona

Dear Elder Hewitt,

I hope you get this by Christmas. I made this peanut brittle and was going to send it regular mail, but I found out you probably wouldn't get it until February! So I sent it airmail—you got a FEW less pieces than you would have gotten! I couldn't believe how much this cost to send! Oh, well, it was my Christmas deed. I was going to buy a Christmas for a needy family until I had to send this airmail, so the needy family is going to have to wait until next Christmas!

I'm joking!

I enjoyed your letter! That's more like it! You really are pretty good with your descriptions. Maybe you ought to major in English! Just for the heck of it I stopped off at the library to see what they had on Sydney. I found a map and a picture portfolio. You're right, it's beautiful! I even found Turramurra! There were a lot of pictures of their beaches. You seemed quite aware of what was going on in that part of Sydney, I must say! I hope you are keeping your mind on your work!

Just joking again—I'm sure you are.

I am looking forward to Christmas. I've been embroidering some pillowcases for my grandparents, and I'm excited to see Grandma's reaction when she sees what I've done! We are going to their place in Bountiful for the holidays. It's been snowing up there, so I plan on getting in a little skiing, too. It doesn't feel at all like Christmas here in Tempe at our 60 to 70 degrees, so I can imagine how strange it would feel if it were the middle of summer like where you are!

I've decided I mustn't play favorites here in the missionary letter writing business, so I'm going to send a letter and the peanut brittle I couldn't send to you to your friend Errol. I hear from the locals that he's a pretty sharp guy. I don't know his folks very well. For some reason or other I haven't seen them at church too much in the last month or two. Somebody said they were having some financial problems or at least some kind of problems. I hope it's nothing too serious.

Well, I'd better end this so I can get my C.A.R.E. package off to your buddy.

> *Merry Christmas!*
> *Becky*
> *(or "Enid" if Becky*
> *bothers you so much!)*

P.S. Sorry about the quality of the picture—it's the only "spare" one I had. The other girl in the picture is my friend Anna. We have a couple of classes together at ASU. She's not LDS, but I'm trying!

o—꜀ꜱꜱꜱꝏ⟩⭒

December 29, 1961
Turramurra, NSW

Dear Errol,

I haven't heard from you in quite awhile, and I hope everything is okay. This time of year here, everything slows to a crawl! Christmas Day was interesting! It started off with a phone call from the roommates of one of our investigators. There are four Maori girls from New Zealand living together and working here in Sydney. Three of them are LDS and the other one, Pua, we are teaching. Anyway, I guess Pua had a heart attack, and we zoomed over there to give her a blessing. (We got a car the other day! The mission bought ten Ford Anglias—an Australian made car, and we got one of them! What a difference it makes! This driving on the left side though is scare-ry!) Well, we got over there, and they had already taken Pua to the hospital so we drove there and gave her a blessing. I think she is going to be okay, and she really seemed grateful that we came. We had her scheduled for baptism in two weeks and hopefully we can go ahead with it.

Then Elder Brandon and I did a little sight seeing. We went to the Sydney Botanical Gardens and took some pictures. It was like a well kept up tropical jungle! After that, we went to a Koala bear sanctuary. That's the only place you can find those bears anymore. Finally we went back to our "mansion" for Christmas tea (dinner) and did we ever get fed! We stuffed ourselves! I think this was the first day since I got over my appendicitis deal that we haven't been out actually proselyting, and we both felt a little guilty. Stuffed and comfortable and a little guilty!

I got another letter and some really good peanut brittle from Becky. She said she was going to send some to you, too. She also sent me a picture of her. The problem is, there were two girls in the picture. One is really cute! I mean, *really* cute. The other one looks, well, I would say, "average minus." She didn't bother to tell me which one she is! I got to figure out a tactful way of finding out which one she is. If she's the real cute one, I'll tell her you really don't like to write letters, and she can direct all of her letter writing efforts my way. If she's the other one, I'll build you way up and put a lot of distance between my letters to her—like ten months! Ha! One thing's for sure, she makes good peanut brittle!

You are really on the downhill now. You've got less than eight months left. That's not very long! I didn't think I'd ever think this, but I'm glad you are the one who came out earlier instead of me! In fact, I've been wondering if I could extend my mission another month or two. I briefly mentioned it to the mission president the other day. He said there wasn't too much chance, but to bring it up again when I had two or three months left.

Well, I'd better end this. By the way, Becky said something about your folks having some financial problems or something. I hope everything is okay!

Love,
Pete

o——ᴀᴜᴜᴜ ⅄

January 3, 1962
Turramurra, NSW

Dear Becky,

Hey, thanks for the goodies and the letter! They were great! I felt a little guilty about eating it knowing that it represented some needy family's Christmas, but it was either eat it or watch it disappear into Elder Brandon's mouth!

Look, about your name, I really don't have any problems with "Becky." I just like "Enid," too. Thanks for the picture of you and your friend, too. Those are two nice looking young women, but you forgot to tell me which one was you. Do you have on the red sweater or the brown one?

I hope you had a good Christmas in the snow. We just visited a botanical garden (don't ask me to describe it—the only plant's name I know is "dandylion"!) and a Koala bear sanctuary. Those bears are really cute, but they aren't as cuddly as they look. Their long black claws aren't just for looks and are as sharp as razors! They let me hold one, but I had on leather gloves and a canvas coat! We had a tremendous dinner at our place afterwards, including roast goose! This place we live at is a boarding house for rich people. The owner

92

gave us a super deal because of our great looks, our pleasant personalities, our sense of humor and our conversational skills! Being two broke American missionaries that the owner (a sixty-year-old woman) wanted to mother didn't hurt either!

Believe me, the rest of the places I have stayed on my mission aren't like this! This has been a great area. We have already seen a number of baptisms and have a lot of people we're teaching. I love this work! To see how people's lives change is worth any sacrifice I have had to make. A lot of people talk about our sacrifices, but I can't honestly say I've done much sacrificing, if any! I'm not saying I haven't had some hard times, but in a real sense they have been some of my biggest blessings. I hope you can understand what I'm trying to say. I just don't want to be anywhere else than right here!

For example, we've got this one kid we're teaching. He's the laziest and most socially backwards kid I've ever seen. He even *lays* down on his couch while we're giving him the discussions! His mom is divorced and works to support him. He is sixteen and has never had a job and has been out of school since he was fourteen. Most kids quit school then and start working but not Ned! He just lays around his house eating and watching TV and playing with his dog. Anyway, he has responded well to the lessons. It's hard to keep from laughing sometimes, though. When we first started teaching him, we wanted to show him how to pray so we explained you start the prayer by saying, "Our Heavenly Father," then we thank Him for the things we have and ask Him for the things we need and want, then we close in the name of Jesus Christ. Then we asked him what he was thankful for. He thought for a minute and just shrugged his shoulders. We suggested maybe he was thankful for us teaching him the gospel. He nodded his head up and down and said, "Yah, yah." Then we asked him what he would like to ask his Heavenly Father for. He just sat there for a long time and finally said, "Maybe I could ask Him to help me teach Butch some new tricks." He was serious! I about fell off my chair! That was his prayer!

He is scheduled for baptism tomorrow, and we were over to his place tonight. He was really nervous about being baptized, and we were trying to calm him down. Finally, we suggested that we have a prayer to help him and that each one of us would take a turn. He said okay. I started off, then Elder Brandon took his turn, then we all knelt there waiting for Ned. Neither Elder Brandon nor I would look up, and I know Ned was looking at us hoping we would do something to help him. But we figured he could do it on his own. Finally he said, "Dear God, please give me the guts to go through with this baptism. Amen." At first I felt like laughing. Then I opened my eyes and looked at Ned, and he was shaking and I could see tears in his eyes. I just looked at him, and I kept thinking about the change that was coming over him and what a blessing the Church was going to be in his life. Elder Brandon and I both were doing some "fast blinking." (You'll find out sooner or later that I sometimes have a problem keeping my eyes dry!) It was great, and he's going to be baptized tomorrow for sure!

Well, I'd better stop rambling here and get some sleep. Thanks again for the candy and the picture—which ever one you are!

Sincerely,
Elder Hewitt

P.S. You're right (or I should say the "locals" are right) about Errol. He's as sharp as they come! I'm sure he will enjoy hearing from you—especially the candy!

o—◦◦◦◦◦ ⟩⟨

January 9, 1962
Oakland, Calif.

Dear Pete,

Sorry I haven't written, but I told you I would be busy. It's good to hear you are doing some baptizing. I got a letter and candy from Becky. I answered her back. You're right, it's good! There's not much new to report here, really, just the same old stuff. It's hard to believe I'll be home in eight months. In answer to your question about my dad, things have been a little slow in the house building business, but that always happens—especially this time of year.

Keep up the good work.

Errol

o——————⟩⋆

January 10, 1962
Tempe, Arizona

Dear Peter,

I got tired of calling you Elder Hewitt! And speaking of names, I'll let you know when I'm ready to be called Enid rather than Becky. In the meantime, let's just leave it at Becky, okay?

You're welcome for the candy! From the sound of things— the place you live in, going around to gardens and koala bear reserves, watching the girls on the beach and all—I believe you when you say you aren't making a lot of sacrifices! That's not quite like the missions I've read about!

Your "Ned" sounds interesting to say the least! It really must be exciting to see that kind of a change in people. I've thought about going on a mission. I wish they would lower the age for the women! Having to wait until you're 22 virtually insures your spinsterhood! I'm nineteen-plus now, and that's nearly three years away—who knows! One thing is for certain—I'm going to finish college, and neither marriage nor mission is going to stop me!

I envy you, though. I can almost feel what you were feeling when Ned said that prayer. I already have a strong testimony of the gospel, but I wish I could have experiences like that. Thank you for sharing it with me. By the way, I don't think it's so bad that a boy or a man cries! I can't stand these guys that go around all tough and machoistic. Like there is some sort of stereotyped image that all girls have to have and all boys have to have! Some of these guys at ASU, especially all the football players, like to pretend they are men! With their grunts, crude talk and heads sitting on their shoulders—none of them has a neck!—they more resemble gorillas! That may be appealing to the flighty cheerleaders around here—all neck and no heads!—but I find it quite repulsive!

As you can tell, I have opinions and am sometimes known to express them. I choose to think I am honest and unafraid to speak out. Dad says I have a chronic case of "Hoof and Mouth" disease!

I received a letter from your friend Errol. I am impressed! From the sound of things, he certainly has been an outstanding missionary and leader! I made the same promise to him as I did to you—I'll answer every letter, but that's it! I really feel sorry for his folks. From what Dad says—he's in the high priest quorum with Errol's dad—I guess their business went bankrupt and they've put their house up for sale and are moving into an apartment. I guess their oldest daughter and her baby are living with them, too. Apparently she's divorcing her husband. It is really sad how this all has affected them. They haven't been out to church for over four months now and appear to be totally inactive. I can imagine how devastated Errol must be about their inactivity. He really must be something else, though, because he didn't even let on to me in his letter that there were any problems at home!

Well, I'd better get back to some studying. By the way, I

had a terrific Christmas vacation. I spent most of it skiing—
at Alta.

Sincerely,
Becky

P.S. About the picture I sent, I forgot what color of sweater I was wearing. Since you thought both of us were "nice looking" girls, it really doesn't matter that much which one is me anyway does it?

o———◦

January 23, 1962
Turramurra, NSW

Dear Errol,

Thanks for your letter. I also got one from Becky. Listen, she told me about the problems your folks are having. I think I know a little bit how you feel. I wish there were some way that I could take some of the load off you. I just want you to know that I love you, and I think that you and your family are the greatest! You have been such an inspiration to me, and I appreciate that. Listen, if you want to talk about it, you know that anything you tell me I'll keep to myself. If you'd rather not, that's okay, too. I just want you to know that nothing's changed as far as how I think about your family. Those things happen to everybody! Becky told me she had received a letter from you, and she went on and on about what a great guy you were! I couldn't agree more!

Our area here is still going great. We baptized that Maori girl I was telling you about last week and a young married couple that one of the members introduced us to in November. I just can't get over what a thrill it is to watch these people change!

I've got to tell you about this one thing that happened two

weeks ago. We've been teaching this fifteen year old boy since November, too. He's an only child and his dad is over sixty and his mom is in her late fifties. Anyway, he has been coming out to everything—church, MIA, the youth dances and stuff, but has been putting off his baptism until his mother is well enough to see it. She is asthmatic and has been in the hospital for the last six weeks! Neither her nor her husband wanted to be taught, because they said they were "too old to change"! But they were all for John being baptized. They had known some of John's Mormon friends for quite awhile and were all for him being like that!

This asthma thing with her has been something else. She has had the thing seriously for the last twenty years, and I guess has come near to dying a lot of times. She is so bad that I guess the doctor told her she has to have the hair dresser shampoo her hair so they can dry it fast with the big hair dryer to keep her from catching cold. She can only bathe once a week, and I guess that is more a sponge bath. Anyway, a week or so ago, the doctor told John and his dad that his mother would never come out of the hospital alive this time. John was pretty shook up when he told us about it. While he was telling us, I had this real funny feeling come over me like I had to tell him about the power of the priesthood! So I did. I told him we had the power to heal his mother. Elder Brandon was just staring at me, and I was wondering myself what I just got through saying. John just said, "That's great! Let's go tell Mom!" It was like there was no question or anything. We could heal her and that was that!

We took John to the hospital and up to his mother's room. Actually, it was a ward, and there were fifteen or twenty beds in there. His mom really looked bad. She was hooked up to the oxygen, and there were these tubes in her arm, and she was just laying there hardly breathing and wheezing so heavily that you wondered how any air was getting to her lungs at all. We asked her how she was feeling, and then John said, "Mom, the elders have the priesthood. That means they can heal you.

Do you want them to?" She just nodded her head yes.

We pulled the curtains around her bed, and Elder Brandon anointed her and I blessed her. I was trying to think of all of these words to say, but my mind was totally blank, except I kept getting this feeling to bless her that she would recover fully. So that's what I said. It must have been the shortest blessing in the history of the Church! She smiled and said thank you, and we pulled the curtains back and left.

Three days later, she was home from the hospital! The doctor couldn't figure out what happened, and she feels better than she has in twenty years! We are baptizing John in three days, and both of his folks will be there, and we gave them both the first discussion last night! She said, "I wonder if the doctor will let me be baptized?" Errol, I just don't understand why I am being blessed with these experiences!

You're my best friend, Errol, and I feel so bad about your folks and what you're going through. I wish there were some way I could help. You know you are in my prayers!

Love,
Pete

P.S. Remember those two elders in my district I told you about that were having some problems? They are leading my district so far this month in proselyting hours, Books of Mormon passed out and meetings held. They have already had one baptism and are expecting another one before the end of the month! They are great! Talk about a change! It's thrilling!

P.P.S. I still haven't found out which one Becky is in the picture she sent me. I'm getting a little worried though. She seems to be purposely avoiding the question, and that can probably mean only one thing—she's the "wrong" one! I must admit I like her letters, though!

Dear Becky,

You certainly don't have to call me Elder Hewitt, but if you'll call me Pete, instead of Peter, I'll call you Becky instead of Enid. Only Mom calls me Peter. Does that sound like a mother?

I have noticed in your letters that you have a tendency to beat around the bush. Wouldn't it be better if you came right out and said what you meant? Ha!

By the way, for your information, the only time I'm near the beach is when we go to visit my elders there, and that's been only three times since I moved to Sydney. I can assure you that when we've been down there, the beach and what's on it has been Elder Brandon's and my least concern. We didn't even notice it was there! Well, hardly.

I will have to admit, though, I may have been "frivolous" as far as visiting gardens and animal sanctuaries. After all, I've done that every Christmas! I realize I've been totally out of line here, and I promise that next Christmas I won't do it!

With respect to your picture, although both of you are "nice looking" girls, you certainly aren't twins, and it would still be nice to know what you look like—not that it matters that much, as you say.

Things are going great here! This is such an exciting place to be. Two of the elders in my district who had had some problems have got their act together and are really doing well. That is almost as exciting as seeing someone accept the gospel! Speaking of which, remember Ned? Well, we baptized him and the next week he had a job! No kidding! He went out and got a job, and he actually sits up when we go out to see him and his mother! In fact, she was so amazed at what has happened here she asked us to give her the lessons!

By the way, I appreciate that information about Errol's folks. He hadn't said anything and probably wouldn't have.

He is such a dedicated elder that he would have just kept it to himself and just kept on going. I wish there was some way I could help him. I know it's got to be a burden on him. I'm just wondering about his finances now. The ward would step in here, wouldn't they? I mean I'm sure the bishop or the high priest quorum or somebody would help here, wouldn't they? If it wouldn't be too much trouble, maybe you could ask your dad or somebody. I'd sure appreciate it! We've got to do everything we can to keep this from being a big worry and burden on Errol.

I really enjoy your letters and am looking forward to seeing you in person in nine months or so—unless I get the extension I am asking for! You'd better have your friend with you, though, or I probably won't recognize you!

> *Sincerely,*
> *Elder Hewitt*
> *(Pete)*

P.S. I played football at ASU my freshman year, and my sister Janice was a varsity cheerleader that same year. What do you think the genetic probabilities are of a "no-neck" and an "all-neck" coming from the same family?

o———ᴔᴔᴔᴔ⟩⊁

> February 5, 1962
> Tempe, Arizona

Dear "Pete,"

Now you know why my dad says I have "Hoof and Mouth"! I apologize for my remarks about football players and cheer-leaders—at least my all-inclusive generalization about football players and cheerleaders. I have seen your picture at your home, and I could see you definitely have a neck. At least you had a tie on, and I assume that went around a neck!

101

With respect to your "beach activities," me thinketh you protest too loudly! There's nothing to be ashamed of! I'm sure a young man who has been on a mission for the better part of a year and a half might be excused for looking at a girl every once in a while. The only problem that that might cause is making some girl friend at home jealous. Of course, that may be a serious problem with you, I don't know! Your being a big football star and all, you may have some little cheerleader around here breathlessly waiting your return and for her to think that your eye was even caught momentarily by "another woman," might be absolutely devastating to the poor thing! Not to mention the thoughts of you extending your mission! That might be just enough for her to decide to pack it in and go looking for game a little closer to home! In any case, please don't feel that you have to explain anything to me. And I think it would be absolutely great if you could extend your mission! (Do you think there is much chance you will?)

Wow! That was magnanimous of you to vow not to go to "gardens and animal sanctuaries" this next Christmas—of course you'll be home!

Seriously, I can tell you are a very good missionary, and I really appreciate you telling me your experiences. I hope you don't mind my joking around. Sometimes I'm actually serious, but usually it is carefully camouflaged. Maybe that can be your little challenge—to try to figure out when I am!

I talked to my dad about Errol's folks and Errol's financial situation. He said the high priest quorum had volunteered to the bishop to finance the rest of Errol's mission. The bishop was going to talk to Errol's dad about it and then to Errol, so that looks to be all taken care of. Dad said that Errol's father seems to be pretty bitter about the Church. I guess he figured that since he was a full tithe payer that if the Church were true, his bankruptcy and all wouldn't have happened. That's a pretty good question. What do you think?

Well, I've got to get back to my studies. I also need to write a letter to Errol. I got one from him the same day I got yours.

He still didn't say anything about his family's problems, and it was pretty short.

By the way, regarding that picture I sent, I am about two inches taller than Anna—but come to think of it, I can't remember whether Anna was standing on the step behind us or not. If she was, then she would look taller than me. If she wasn't, then I would be the taller one. I'll try to remember if she was or wasn't!

Keep up the great work!

Yours truly,
Becky

o——ααιιο)ɤ

February 7, 1962
Parramatta, NSW

Dear Errol,

Well, I got another transfer and another companion. I sure hated leaving Elder Brandon—that was my best companionship yet! He was made a senior when I left. He was certainly ready! My new companion is Elder Strong from Camden, New Jersey. Well, I'm back in the real world of missionaries! The place we're staying at doesn't quite resemble where I just came from. We live in a regular home owned by this lady who is probably in her sixties. She is just a "little" different! For one thing, she's going bald! There is a real old man living here, too, and we have to cook for ourselves! I haven't had to do that since the first four months of my mission!

Parramatta is about thirty miles west of downtown Sydney and a little further south than Turramurra. The country is pretty flat out here, but it is still beautiful. We're quite close to the "bush," and it's not unusual to see a wild kangaroo hop across the road when you drive further west.

I hope everything is going okay with you and your family,

Errol. I haven't heard from you for awhile, and I hope things are getting better for you. Write when you can.

Love,
Pete

P.S. We baptized the elderly parents of that boy I was telling you about in my last letter. His mother's doctor advised her against "getting all wet" because of her asthma, but everything just went fine. Boy, was she happy! It was mighty!

o———aooo╱x

February 14, 1962
Parramatta, NSW

Dear Becky,

Thanks for your letter and your apology is accepted! I can assure you I do have a neck! Actually, I was a defensive back and one of the "smaller" guys on the team! By the way, I admit I do look at a girl every once in awhile, and, no, I don't have a "cheerleader" waiting for me. You also asked about my extending my mission. I don't know what the deal on that is yet. President Cook, my mission president, said there was a possibility, but with the increasing number of missionaries coming out now, not very probable.

I'm kind of curious why you seem interested in if I have a girl waiting for me or if I'm going to get an extension.

Well, as you can see by my new address, I've been transferred. Parramatta is a Sydney suburb about 30 miles due west of the downtown. My new companion, Elder Strong, is from New Jersey and is a "good head"! We are working closely with the teenagers in the Church out here and already have some exciting things happening. The ward out here is great! These kids are about as gung-ho for missionary work as I have ever seen.

We already have a family scheduled for baptism, and we've only been meeting with them for a week and a half. It's a whole family, too! They have two teenagers and three smaller children—all over eight! We met the family when we first moved here. The older kids had been coming out to the dances and had been telling their parents what they had been learning at Church. The whole family came out to church with us last Sunday! We are to baptize them on the 27th of this month.

You were "complaining" about how "easy" I was having it. Well, all that has changed. This place we are living at now is not quite what I've been used to the last year. For one thing, we've got to do our own cooking. I could stand to lose a few pounds anyway! We've been so busy that we haven't taken time to do more than heat up a can of soup or eat cold cereal and milk. To be truthful, time has nothing to do with it—that's the extent of our cooking skills!

Our landlady, Mrs. McClaren, is interesting to say the least. We actually live in a spare bedroom in her house. She is in her sixty's and is WILD! Actually, what I mean by that is she is drunk most of the time! It is sad, but sometimes it's funny, too. She is a widow and works night shift at a local hospital as a nurse. She is generally pretty sober by the time she has to go to work.

Apparently she used to be very wealthy. Her husband and she owned a huge plantation in Indonesia somewhere before World War II broke out. They came directly from Scotland and developed thousands of acres of land there. They had servants and everything. Then when World War II broke out and the Japanese were taking over the whole Far East, they had to leave everything and get out. Her husband died a short time later, and she moved here to Australia and of course lost everything. It's almost like she quit wanting to live, with her booze and all. She is really nice, though, and seems to like us. She refuses to call us "Elder" and insists on calling us by our first names. She's kind of a funny looking old duck. She is nearly bald, and what hair she does have left is bright red! I think maybe that's why she decided to be a nurse—so she could wear a hat to cover her head!

There is one other renter here, a Mr. Kraft. He is over 80 years old and used to work as a hand on a station (ranch). He is "unusual" too! He has a wooden leg and according to Mrs. McClaren, doesn't want anybody to know it. It's pretty hard not to notice it, though, since it squeeks when he walks! He needs to oil it or something. Anyway, he isn't very talkative and is really grumpy. I guess I would be, too, if I were in that situation.

The other day we were out of sugar, and my companion "borrowed" some that was sitting in a bowl in the cupboard to put on his cereal. As it turned out, it belonged to Mr. Kraft. He about had a stroke when he found out! He was jumping up and down with this sugar bowl in his hand, screaming, "Thief! Thief!" I finally got him calmed down and told him we were sorry and that we would buy him a whole bag. That seemed to settle him down, and he just stood there shaking his head back and forth saying, "If you can't trust a minister, who can you trust!" We had to do everything we could to keep from laughing. That would have been the last thing we needed to do to cement relationships!

Anyway, we bought the sugar for him and since the day of the Great Sugar Robbery he has kept his sugar bowl and his new bag of sugar in his bedroom! He also has a bathing problem. The problem is, he doesn't! At least he hasn't since we've moved here. Mrs. McClaren says it is a real ordeal for him to do it. He has to unscrew his leg (or whatever they do), and it takes him at least three hours to take the bath. I hope he breaks down and does it pretty soon! I can tell you there is no way Mr. Kraft is going to ever sneak up on anybody. That squeek and smell announce his arrival way before you ever see him!

I appreciate you finding out about what the ward is doing

to help Errol financially. That's a relief to know they are already doing something. I don't understand Errol's dad feeling that way about the Church, though. I can see his "logic," but I don't agree with it. I'm certainly not a Joseph Fielding Smith with the scriptures or a President McKay with understanding, and I don't know whether I have an answer for you. But it seems to me the real question is who we want to be and how we want to live. I don't know why his business failed, and maybe that isn't even important. I know we are promised certain things when we live the law of tithing, but I don't think that means we will all be rich or won't have financial problems. It seems to me those promises are more long-term. It just doesn't make sense to me to have a problem and blame the Church for the problem and then stop living the gospel. Maybe the real problem is he doesn't want to live the gospel anymore and his business failure just gave him the excuse. I don't know whether that even makes sense, and I certainly am in no position to judge! I do know Errol is a good man and wants to do what's right, and I feel so sorry for him! I am worried about him, though, and I haven't heard from him in nearly two months.

I really like your letters, Becky, and I appreciate you taking the time to write me. I accept your challenge to figure out when you're serious—and maybe your challenge can be to figure out when I'm joking!

> *Yours truly,*
> *Pete*

P.S. THANKS for the CLUE on the pictures! The girl in the red sweater appears to be a couple of inches taller than the other, but she also might be standing on a step—as you pointed out. Any other clues as to which one you are? You've been a great help so far!

o—aooo⋝

February 20, 1962
Oakland, Calif.

Dear Pete,

Thanks for your letters. I have enjoyed them as usual. As you probably know, my family has had some rather serious problems financially and all. This has been a difficult time for me the last month or so, and I've made a decision to be released from my mission and go home. The bishop told me the ward is prepared to support me, but I don't like to take anything from anybody and that wouldn't be satisfactory to me. The big reason, though, is my family's inactivity. I think that is where my responsibilities are—to help them become active again. So I have talked to my mission president about it, and he will give me an honorable release. I leave for home day after tomorrow.

See you in October and don't worry about me.

Errol

o——oooooo———

February 27, 1962
Tempe, Arizona

Dear Pete,

I guess you heard the news about Errol. I talked to him quite a bit at church Sunday. In fact, he asked me out for this weekend. I feel so sorry for him! He really is a sharp guy. It's a shame he had to leave his mission so early with the great contribution he was making and all. But I really admire him for coming home to work with his family. That had to be a tough thing for him to do! He's going to give his homecoming talk this next Sunday. He said his folks told him they would come out to it so it looks like his decision is paying off already!

As usual, I enjoyed your letter, and I accept your challenge to determine when you're joking! I certainly didn't mean to imply that I thought you thought you owed me explanations about what you were doing. (You missed one there—I was just joking!) It certainly isn't my business nor does it bother me one way or another that you like to look at girls all the time. And please don't get any wrong ideas about why I was wondering about a girlfriend back home and your mission extension. I was just making conversation!

I've been thinking about what you said about Errol's folks and why they might be inactive. It sounded like you were almost saying they were actually choosing not to live the gospel and that choice was their real reason and the bankruptcy and the law of tithing was just an excuse. Was that what you were saying? It's hard for me to imagine that anyone who actually knows the gospel is true would choose to live some other way! I mean I can see it if they never had a testimony, but if they know it's true—I mean REALLY know it's true, wouldn't they always want to live it?

Hey, your present apartment sounds more normal—except for those two housemates of yours! I thought I'd die laughing when I read about Mr. Kraft and the sugar!

I'm glad you like my letters. I REALLY like yours. I almost feel like I'm out there. I know how busy you are and what a sacrifice it is to spend the amount of time you spend writing me. Thanks!

> *Yours truly,*
> *Becky*

P.S. About the picture, I just remembered—my eyes are blue and Anna's are brown! On the other hand, we are probably standing too far away from the camera for you to tell! Oh, well, I'll keep trying to remember which sweater I had on.

February 28, 1962
Parramatta, NSW

Dear Errol,

I just received your letter today. I'm sending this letter to
your mission home because I don't have your home address.
(Becky said your folks had moved.) So I'm hoping they have
the right address and will forward it.

I don't quite know what to say. I was surprised to say the
least! I can understand your reasons for leaving, and I admire
your willingness to give up your mission to help your folks. I
hope it was the right decision for you and that it won't be
something you will regret.

I'm kind of at a loss for words right now, but I just want
you to know I'm thinking about you, and you and your folks
are in my prayers. Please write and let me know your address.

Love,
Pete

o———⟊

March 15, 1962
Mesa, Arizona

Dear Pete,

Thanks for your letter and your concern. I just got it, and I
wanted to get back to you. I don't have any regrets about
leaving my mission early. I figure with what I did it was
equivalent to what most missionaries would have taken three
or four years to do, so I don't have any regrets that way. It
would have been nice to have stayed the whole two years, but
you've got to do what you feel is right and right now I think
my folks need me more than the mission does.

I'm staying with them here in their apartment. As you can
see by the address, they moved out of Tempe into Mesa. My

sister and her baby live here with us so it's kind of crowded. I can't get into school right now since the semester has already started—I don't have any money to do it anyway—so I've gone to work. Dad got me a job as a "rough carpenter" with one of the general contractors he knows so I'm doing that full time. They pay real good money, about $3.25 an hour.

Keep up the good work and don't worry about me. By the way, I met Becky and in fact have taken her out a couple of times. We're getting along really good.

Errol

o——aaaao ɔ̸

March 22, 1962
Parramatta, NSW

Dear Becky,

Sorry it's taken me awhile to get back to you this time. We have been really busy. I got a letter from Errol telling me he was going home just before I got your last letter. I've heard from him since he's been home, and he said you and he had been going out and were getting along really good. Listen, I don't want to be a fifth wheel here or anything. You don't really have to answer this back if you don't want to. It would probably be good if I didn't spend so much time writing letters anyway. There's so much to do here. We're going night and day.

Look, I have appreciated your letters and all and getting to know you and hopefully will get to meet you when I get home in October.

Sincerely,
Elder Hewitt
(Pete)

P.S. I nearly forgot your question. You asked if I thought somebody really knew the Church was true, wouldn't he live it? I certainly am not an expert on doctrine, but it seems to me that everybody has got to know it's true sooner or later—either here or in the spirit world—and everybody has got to make some choices and apparently some are going to choose something different than to be a Celestial person even when they know what everything's all about. I'm sure Satan has no doubt about the Church being true, and he isn't exactly "in the fold"! Of course, this is just my opinion.

Thanks again for your letters over these last three or four months.

◦—◅▥▥▥◦⟩≺

March 22, 1962
Parramatta, NSW

Dear Errol,

The work is really going great here! We participated in four baptisms this last week. All we did was teach; the kids in this ward here did all of the "work"! They are such great examples to their non-member friends and are fantastic missionaries. One of the baptisms was an eighteen-year-old girl who had been coming out to church for three years steady but couldn't be baptized before because her father wouldn't give permission. The other three were a mother and her two children. She's divorced, and her thirteen-year-old has been coming out to church. We asked the mother for permission to teach her daughter, and the mother asked if we would mind letting her listen in! We said we could probably arrange that! Anyway, she was baptized along with her daughter and her ten-year-old son! This mission is so great!

We've still got a hopper full, too. One guy we're meeting with is a lay minister for the Baptist church. He is only a couple of years older than we are but is really knowledgeable.

112

At first he was belligerent, but now (we've given him four discussions) he asks the neatest questions and reads everything we give him and has been coming out to church. He will be a real power!

Well, I'd better get back to work. I'd sure appreciate hearing from you.

Love,
Pete

P.S. I hope everything is okay there with your family. You served a great mission and can be proud of what you did. I hope that this decision to come home early works out like you want it to.

P.P.S. If you have a minute, I'd appreciate you dropping over and seeing Mom. She seemed a little down in her last letter. It's been five months since Dad passed away, and everything is back to "normal" at home, and I think the "emptiness" is just starting to really hit her. I still have to fight sometimes to keep my mind on things.

P.P.P.S. Look, if you're getting something going with Becky and want me to "bug out," let me know. Like I told her in my last letter, I don't want to get in anybody's way here.

o—∞∞≻

March 28, 1962
Tempe, Arizona

Dear "Elder Hewitt,"

I am going to accept your challenge to determine when you are joking and assume the last letter you wrote was a big joke! If it wasn't, it was the stupidest letter I've ever read! Listen, if you don't want to write to me, just say so. You certainly don't have to! But don't you go telling me how I feel and who I'm in love with and who's a "fifth wheel" and don't you go making

113

assumptions as to who I want to write to and what going on a couple of dates with Errol means! You ought to know me well enough by now to know I'll tell you how I feel! And I happen to feel that Errol is a real nice guy, and he's been fun to be with. I also happen to think you're okay, too—maybe a little dumb, but okay. And maybe even a little more than "okay." At least that's how I felt up until I received your really DUMB letter! In any case, I'm certainly not on the verge of being "swept off my feet" by anybody, and I can go out with who I want, and I can write to whomever I want!

To quote someone you know very well, "You don't really have to answer this back if you don't want to!" My promise still holds. I'll answer every letter you send, so it's up to you whether this continues!

Sincerely,
Sister Wingate
(Becky)

P.S. I'm the one in the red sweater.

o—aww⟩t

April 3, 1962
Parramatta, NSW

Dear Becky,

My hands are still burning from handling your letter! I deserved it, and I'm sorry! I guess it really was a dumb letter I sent. I wasn't thinking too well, and I just didn't want to rock anybody's boat or anything. Thank you for writing back. I would have really missed your letters if they had stopped! I feel flattered to think that you think I might be even better than "okay"! I think you are an "okay" yourself! At least!

By the way, I already knew you were wearing the red sweater. It was a matter of logic. Knowing Errol like I do, I knew he would never have asked your brown-sweatered friend out. To be honest, I probably wouldn't have either if I just met her at church or something. It's interesting, though, after writing to you these last few months and getting your letters back, I wasn't anywhere near as concerned which girl you were as I was when I first got the picture. That's the truth for what it's worth.

Well, back to my mission! It is tremendous! I just don't see how it could get any better. I keep waiting for something negative or bad to happen, but it doesn't. Sometimes I think that maybe the Lord is grouping my experiences together. The first part of my mission was really hard for me. It was just one difficult experience after another, and I didn't feel like I was accomplishing anything. But since Dad's death and my appendectomy, it has been like I always dreamed a mission would be! I know it isn't me. At least I don't think it is. I don't seem to be doing anything too much different than I was doing before, except hopefully I'm a little wiser and more patient. Judging from my last letter to you, I would have to conclude that even that's not the case!

Sometimes I think this is happening to me because of Dad. Sometimes I think the Lord is blessing me because of what a good man my dad was, and this is His way of rewarding him. That is a humbling thought, and I don't think it's too far off the mark!

We've got two more baptisms scheduled for tomorrow night. We are going to hold the baptism after our youth group meeting. One night a week we give a discussion to the non-member kids the youth in our ward bring to this group meeting. Usually, we have anywhere from fifteen to twenty LDS kids there and up to a half dozen of their non-member friends. One of the baptisms is a fourteen-year-old young man who has been coming to the meetings. The other is a "former" lay Baptist preacher. He is great and is definitely going to be a big asset to the ward. We have a font at the chapel, but Don (the "preacher") wanted to be baptized like the Savior, in a

115

river. So we got permission to do it in the Parramatta River. That will be exciting!

Our "housemates" as you called them continue to be interesting! Mr. Kraft finally took a bath! Mrs. McClaren was right—it took him almost four hours! I had to drive down to the service station to go to the bathroom! Believe me, it was worth the sacrifice!

He really got mad at us a couple of weeks ago. He has this little pet parakeet, and ever since we got here he's been trying to make the bird say "Mr. Kraft." The bird wouldn't give him the time of day! We thought we would try to make it talk, so every time we passed by the bird (as long as Mr. Kraft wasn't in the room), we would say "Jock's a Mormon"! The bird's name is Jock, of course. Anyway, two weeks ago, Mr. Kraft was trying to get it to say "Mr. Kraft," and it screeched, "Jock's a Mormon"! I thought he would die! Since that time he sits in front of the bird and keeps repeating "Jock's a Methodist"! So far, Jock's still a Mormon! That's one convert I've had that seems to be holding!

Well, we felt a little bad about how mad it made Mr. Kraft, so we started teaching Jock another phrase. He finally learned it and said it while Mr. Kraft was in there trying to convert him back to being a Methodist. Jock said, "I love you, Mr. Kraft"! Mr. Kraft just started to weep! He came running (well, hobbling and squeeking) into our room and said, "Did you just hear what Jock said?! He said, 'I love you, Mr. Kraft!' My budgie (that's Aussie for parakeet) said he loved me!" He was just sobbing, and my companion and I looked at each other and started to tear up ourselves. He is one lonely man! We felt lousy for the way we have teased him! We almost considered teaching Jock to say "I'm a Methodist," but we figured the only way Jock was able to say "I love you, Mr. Kraft" was because he was a Mormon! So we are leaving the bird alone from now on!

Mrs. McClaren, our landlady, has been something else! She went for ten days without being sober once! She insisted on washing my socks in this little washing machine of hers, and so I let her. Big mistake! She took all of my socks except the pair I had on and put them in the washing machine. That's where they stayed for three days! Every night when we came home I'd ask her where the socks were, and she would say in the washing machine. I'd take them out and rinse them out and hang them on the line to dry, but they were always wet in the morning so I would have to leave them on the line. Everyday while we were gone, Mrs. McClaren would gather them off the line and put them back in the washing machine again! The socks I was wearing were smelling so bad I didn't even notice Mr. Kraft anymore! She finally sobered up and got them dry! I thought I was going to have to go buy a week's worth of new socks! (And you said it didn't sound like I was doing much sacrificing out here!)

This has been a long one! I guess the relief of getting another letter from you was so great I didn't know when to stop writing! There's more than just a little truth to that statement!

As ever,
Pete

P.S. Mom has been a little depressed lately. Anything you could do or say to cheer her up would be appreciated. Thanks!

o———ᨈ᷒ᨈ᷒᷒ᨆ

April 5, 1962
Mesa, Arizona

Dear Pete,

Thanks for your letter. I'm sure I made the right decision about coming home. I haven't made as much progress with my folks as I would have liked, but I'm trying. One problem is I have to work a lot of Sundays so I can't invite them out to church with me. I don't like that, but it's something I've got to do if I want this job.

It's funny, but my mission seems so unreal to me now. It's been nearly a month and a half since I've come home, and it feels like I never even went on a mission. I've received a letter from my mission president since coming home but nobody else. Oh, well, it's time to get on with life.

I've changed my plans about college quite a bit. I'm not planning to go to BYU anymore. For one thing I can't afford to, but I don't think I want to go there anyway. I've been in an "all church" environment for a year and a half, and I think I'm ready to try the "real" world. So I'm planning to go to ASU part-time in the summer and then full-time in the fall. The guy I'm working with said he'd let me work around school.

I've been seeing a lot of Becky lately. We make a pretty good couple, if I do say so myself. I think she likes me, but I'm not sure whether or not I'm ready to get serious. If and when I do decide to get serious with her, I get the feeling that she would be ready to be serious, too. My parents really like her, and she seems to like them a lot, too. I don't have any objections to you writing to her. I'm sure your letters to her are just like you write to me anyway. Aren't they? I'll keep you up to date about our relationship.

Keep up the good wrork.

"Civilian" Errol

P.S. I've been real busy and haven't had a chance to see your mother yet. I don't know when I'll get over there, but I'll keep trying.

◦———◊

April 10, 1962
Tempe, Arizona

Dear Pete,

I'm glad your hands weren't burned so bad you couldn't write back! Thanks for the letter. I am probably going to regret saying this, but I was worried I wouldn't hear from you again. Don't get me wrong—I'm sure I could have survived it, but I'm glad I didn't have to try! I guess I should take it as a compliment that you rate me an "okay+"! Somehow it doesn't sound exactly "A," but I'll take it.

Well, Sherlock, it's interesting how you figured out which girl I was in the picture. You must know Errol better than I do. What makes you so sure he wouldn't have dated the girl in the brown sweater? And what makes you so sure that I wasn't just joking when I said I was the one in the red? Just something for you to mull around.

Hey, don't be so modest about your successes! I'm sure you have *something* to do with them. I mean, you've got to be working or you won't see anybody to teach! You've got to be studying, or you won't know what to teach! And I'm sure you couldn't have the Spirit with you like I'm sure you do unless you were doing something right! I can understand your feelings about your dad and all, but give yourself some credit, too!

I've been thinking quite a bit about what you said in your letter before last about knowing the gospel is true and making a choice not to live it. I can't argue against your logic—certainly Satan knows it and as you put it, "He is not in the fold!" But I'm confused, too. It seems that all the emphasis in the Church is to try to gain a testimony and then when you do, everything falls into place. When I see somebody like Errol's folks do what they did, I have just assumed that they never really had a testimony, and they were active in church and all because they hoped it would lead them to know, but they never really knew, and that's why when something went wrong they went inactive.

119

But what you're saying is that maybe they know it's true, and they just don't want to live it, and they don't want to admit that to themselves so they make up reasons for not living it. And what that means, I think, is that some—and maybe an awful lot—of the active members of the Church really aren't doing what they want to do and would stop being active and "doing what's right" if they had an excuse—like going bankrupt or something.

If you're right, Pete, that's really scary! I mean maybe *I* don't really want to live it! I think I do, but maybe I don't! Maybe if something came up like a bankruptcy with me, maybe I would do the same thing as Errol's folks. If you're right, that means you can't really tell what another person is like by what he has done before or even by what he is doing now, and maybe the only person who can tell what he is like and what he wants is that person. And maybe he doesn't even know until the *right* event, like a bankruptcy, comes up and he makes this decision! And if that's the case, I don't know whether *YOU* really want to do what's right or whether *ERROL* wants to do what's right (or WANTED to do what's right when he came home from his mission), and how would you know whether who you marry is one who REALLY wants to do what's right! What's even more disturbing, I don't really know whether *I* want to do what's right! I mean, I really don't! Here I sit, for years being the *one* who has all of the *right* answers in Sunday School class, and I don't even know the answer to "Who am I?" I've been thinking about this, and I've been trying to dig inside me to find out and I honestly don't know! Before you get too concerned about me, though, I intend to go right on doing what I'm doing! I *think* that is what I want.

Well, that's enough deep thought for me today! It sounds like you have an ultra-efficient "housemother" there, making sure you have *clean* socks! I'm glad you guys have decided to stop teasing Mr. Kraft. I felt so sorry for him when his bird told him he was a Mormon! It was also pretty funny!

Thanks again for keeping up with the letter writing. You're back to "okay and maybe a little more" in my book! At least!

Yours truly,
Becky

P.S. I went over to your house a couple of times this last week. Your mother is something else! She didn't seem very "down" to me! In fact, the last time I went over, we started talking about the choir number for Sunday, and I ended up playing the piano while your mother sang. I think we went all through that "Pop Songs of World War II" book she has!

o—⚓︎

April 17, 1962
Parramatta, NSW

Dear Becky,

I'm glad I'm back to "okay and a little more" with you! I'm also glad you want me to continue writing. If it's okay with you, though, I'm not going to worry a whole lot about which sweater you were wearing in the picture.

I can see you've been doing some thinking about what I said about choice and testimony! I also agree that when all is said and done, only I can determine what I want to do and who I want to be. But I think, too, you sort of know what you want all along. I mean, I guess you can fool yourself for awhile but not for long. I think deep down inside, you know *why* you're doing what you're doing. I think some keep the commandments because they're afraid of being punished by God if they don't.

I think others do it because they are afraid that people will think negatively about them if they don't. I also think there

121

are some who do it to get praise and recognition and maybe even do it to deceive and get power. But none of these people really WANT to live the commandments, and I think at least deep down inside them they know that! They don't really LOVE the gospel, and they don't really want that to be their way of life. But sooner or later everybody has got to come face to face with himself, and maybe it takes a bankruptcy or a gross sin or a father's death or some other serious problem to force us to really take a look at ourselves. When we come to that moment of our lives, we make the choice we really want to make. We may look for things to rationalize that choice so others will think better of us, but we end up living the kind of life we want to live. At least this is what I think.

I had an experience when I found out my dad was going to die, and I learned some truths about myself. Maybe when I get home in October, I can share that experience with you. (I will be coming home my regular scheduled time because my mission president said there was no way to get an extension.) In the meantime, I'm going to pull your own sweater game on you and let you try to figure out what I discovered about myself!

You've got a point about not knowing whether or not the one you marry has the same righteous desires you have. The only thing I can think of is that we should be able to ask the Lord for revelation about that. That's a tough question, and that may not be a very good answer. I don't know. But I've got to think that if we are in tune, and we ask, we should get an answer. That's my sermon for the day!

You might be interested to know that my "ultra-efficient housemother" has been up to her "tricks" again! Both Elder Strong and I had a bunch of our white shirts that needed collars turned. To save some money, when collars get frayed you can unpick the stitching and reverse the collar so the fraying is underneath and then re-sew it. Anyway, I asked Mrs. McClaren if she knew anyone who could turn our collars. She said that she could and insisted on taking them. (She was sober, or we never would have let her do it!) We got them back last week. They weren't frayed anymore, I will say that much! But she DID NOT turn the collars! What she did was put the shirts in her sewing machine and zig-zagged all over the collars! You can't see any fraying—just stitches all over the collar! The stitching is so thick the collars stand straight up— you can't fold them down over your tie! We've got to use these shirts, though, because they're the only ones we've got, and neither one of us can afford to get new shirts until our monthly checks come from home! In the meantime we look like hoods with ties!

Mr. Kraft has been "interesting," too. He got in a fight with Mrs. McClaren yesterday (they are always arguing!) and said he was going out and jump in the Parramatta River! Mrs. McClaren was all worried (she was drunk!) and came running to our bedroom telling us that Mr. Kraft had left the house and was going to kill himself and insisted we go out and find him! So we did. We went up and down the streets in our car and over to the river and then to his daughter's place—she lives a quarter of a mile from here—but we couldn't find him anywhere so we came back home. By this time Mrs. McClaren was moaning, "I killed him! I killed him!" and was talking about committing suicide herself! We were trying to calm her down when I noticed that Mr. Kraft's bedroom door was shut. I opened it and peeked in, and there he was, laying on his bed sound asleep! He had been there the whole time! Mrs. McClaren stopped moaning and got this smile on her face and said, "Why, that old goat!" and then she passed out!

It is true this flat can't compare to the mansion in Turramurra or Mrs. Voorhees' place in Albury for eating or just about anything else, but it most certainly is NOT boring!

We had a great missionary experience last week, too! We were holding our baptism down at the river after our mission-ary meeting with the kids at the ward. I think I told you we were teaching this former Methodist minister, and he wanted to be baptized in the river. Anyway, we had him and this other young person (a fifteen-year-old girl) scheduled for baptism after the meeting, and we invited everyone there to go to the river to see it. Well, there was this young man, a fourteen-year-old who we had taught at these weekly "group" meetings for the last three weeks, who asked if he could be baptized that night, too. We told him we would have to get his mother's permission (his father was dead), so we called his mother and she said that would be fine so we told her we had to get her signature, and we would be over to get it.

We went to her house and had her sign the permission slip and picked up a change of clothes for Ian (her son). She asked if she could go with us to see it, and of course we were thrilled to have her go. We had to drive about fifteen miles to get to the place where we were holding it, and as we were driving, she was asking questions about the gospel and we were answering them and the Spirit was there as strong as I have ever felt it! I could hardly drive the car I was so weak, and when we got there, I stopped the car and looked at Mrs. Gephart and said, "You know it's true, don't you?" She nodded her head up and down, and I said, "Would you like to be baptized, too?" She looked at me, and she was crying, and she nodded her head up and down again. It was one of the greatest experiences of my life, Becky.

There was a member of the Church that lived about a mile away, and we went and got some "almost" white clothes for Mrs. Gephart, and we baptized them all. It was a little cool and there was "steam" rising out of the water, and we turned the headlights of the car on the river, and it was like we were in heaven with everybody in white and the mist and light and all! I don't think I will ever see another baptism like it!

Becky, I've never told you this before, but there were a lot of times in the first half of my mission that I wanted to go home. I was almost praying I would get sick enough to be sent home "honorably." It seemed like everything was happening to me, and I just didn't feel like I had it in me to stick it out. But if I had gone home, I would have missed that baptism at the river and all the other fantastic experiences I've had, and I would have missed Mrs. McClaren and Mr. Kraft and all these great companions I've had, and I would have missed all that's going to happen in the six months I've got remaining.

I thank God I'm here! For the first part of my mission the days sometimes seemed to drag by. But now, it's like the weeks are days and the months are weeks and before I know it, it'll be time and this whole thing will be over—and I don't want it to be!

Thanks for listening to me and keep the letters coming!

As ever,
Pete

P.S. Thanks for going over to see Mom. She wrote and told me about the singing session. That made her day! Hey, I didn't know you were the accompanist for the choir! Mom said you have played several solos in sacrament meeting. How come you're so modest?!

o———⚬⚬⚬⚬⚬⚬⚬🗲

April 18, 1962
Parramatta, NSW

Dear Errol,

It seems funny writing to you in Mesa rather than in California. My mission is going too fast, and I know another blink or two of my eyes and I will be there with you. I think that's neat you will be going to ASU, and I was thinking maybe we could take some classes together in the fall, but I just remembered I'll get back a little late to start then. Actually, I would like to go to BYU. I think it would be great up there with all those LDS kids. But, like you, I can't afford to.

I'm glad you feel right about your decision to leave your mission early, and I hope you can help your folks. I'm sure it's tough on you to have to work on Sunday. I don't know what I would do in the same situation. I think maybe I'd get another job or something. I really need that uplift I get from church. Maybe I just know how weak I am, I don't know.

Becky and I are still writing to each other, and "yes" my letters to her are pretty much like they are to you. Maybe if I were there, I'd be trying to give you some competition! Ha!

Things are really great here! The Lord has blessed me beyond anything I could ever have dreamed! These people are so tremendous and I have made so many great friends that when the time comes to go, it will be at least as hard for me to leave as it was to come!

Well, I'd better get this in the mail and get getting! Elder Strong and I have got to be into the mission home in an hour. I guess President Cook wants to talk to us about why we're having the success we are with the youth out here. The answer's simple. The kids in the Church here love their friends and want them to be as happy as they are. So they tell them about it! They are great!

> *Love,*
> *Pete*

P.S. Thanks for trying to see Mom. Her last letters sound like her old self again.

o———◦◦◦◦⟩r

> April 26, 1962
> Tempe, Arizona

Dear Pete,

It sounds like your mother laid it on a little thick about my piano playing abilities. Believe me, I'm no Chopin!

I can't believe how fast this year is passing! Another three weeks and I'm out of school! I have been trying to decide whether or not to go to summer school. Dad said I could work for him as a secretary in the English department if I wanted to, and I think that is what I'll do. I could still take some classes I suppose, but I think I'm going to take the summer "off"! It's getting hot already and to think of going to school during that heat is probably more than I can take. Errol is going to go to summer school I guess.

His folks don't seem to be making much progress. I've seen them several times in the last month. They are certainly nice enough, but they don't seem to want to have anything to do with the Church right now. Errol's job requires him to work on Sundays, and that concerns me a little—maybe even more than a little. (Don't tell Errol I said that!) It doesn't seem to bother him, and he feels he can "make up" for it by reading the scriptures and church books on his own. He probably can, but I don't think it's the same thing. Oh, well, it's really none of my business—I guess.

I appreciated your letter and your thoughts about choice and all. I haven't thought much more about it—maybe because I'm afraid to look too deeply into my own heart, I don't know. Perhaps we get so used to doing the church things that we just do them out of habit more than anything else, and we don't want to do any soul searching or any other thought exercise that might "rock the boat" so we just keep on doing our "habit" thing because it's "comfortable." Maybe that's where I am now. At least I'm being honest about it, aren't I?

Sometimes I wish we never started this conversation about choice! I didn't exactly tell the truth a couple of sentences up. Actually, I've *started* to think about this a lot of times, but I try to get it out of my mind because it's so "uncomfortable." I even sort of brought it up once with Errol. I asked him why he thought his folks went inactive. He just kind of snapped back and said if he knew that, they wouldn't be inactive anymore. So I let it drop. He has really taken this thing hard I think. In fact, I think he's so self-conscious about it he doesn't really like to talk about his mission or anything about the Church that much. I have really enjoyed getting to know him, though.

127

He is going to be a success in life without a question! He is articulate, hard working, very intelligent and fun to be around. And there are a few girls in this ward who think he's better looking than Fabian, too! He seems to have it all, doesn't he?

I read that part in your letter about the baptism in the river several times. That must have been a tremendous experience. Since I have been writing to you, you have sounded so enthusiastic and you've had so many neat experiences that it's hard for me to imagine you ever considered coming home early! Do you think Errol regrets coming home early?

Well, I'm going to close this "epistle" off! I'd like to see what this Mrs. McClaren and Mr. Kraft look like. If you've got a minute and a camera and some film, why don't you take a picture of them and send it to me. While you're at it, I wouldn't mind seeing what you look like as a missionary. You're dad was pretty thin on top—how is your hair coming? Out?

Becky

P.S. Are you sure you don't care whether I wear red or brown sweaters?

o——ᴀᴡᴡ✗

May 7, 1962
Wollstencraft, NSW

Dear Becky,

As you can see, I have moved. A couple of weeks ago my companion and I had to go into the mission home to supposedly report on our progress with the youth to my mission president, President Cook. Actually, he talked to me without my companion and only asked me a few questions about the youth in Parramatta. His real purpose was to call me as his second counselor. I don't understand why he chose me, and I don't know whether I ever will. He could see my shock and frankly, I felt so inadequate for that call that I asked him if he was sure of what he was saying. I didn't mean to be rude or ungrateful, I just couldn't imagine me being called as a second counselor! He told me he wasn't saying I was the best missionary in the mission or even the one most qualified for this job and that maybe I was and maybe I wasn't. He went on to say it didn't really matter. That what mattered was the Lord wanted me to serve with him at this time. Then he looked right at me and said I had been called by revelation. I didn't question him anymore.

I've got so much to learn, Becky! I'm just not ready for this kind of calling. At least I don't feel like I am. I can tell you one thing—I can use all the prayers I can get!

This is going to be a beautiful place to live! The mission home is a red brick mansion sitting on top of a slightly sloping hill. There are about two acres of yard in front, and across the street is a heavily wooded park. President and Sister Cook are great people and very humble. President Cook has almost been like a father to me since Dad died. He really lives close to the Lord!

There are two other elders in the mission home besides me, the mission secretary (Elder Grant) and the mission treasurer (Elder Fox). They are both tremendous men, and I'm going to enjoy getting to know them better. The first counselor is the former president of the Brisbane stake and lives with his family up in Brisbane.

I can appreciate your struggles with this choice thing! I wish I could help you, but I don't think I can. What I can say is I feel you are one who loves the Lord and wants to be like Him. I don't know that for sure, but I "feel" it and I believe it. What's more important, perhaps, I *hope* it. I may kick myself for saying this, but when I sent my letter suggesting that you might not want to continue our correspondence, and I thought

I would probably not hear from you again, I was one depressed missionary! I'm glad we are still writing!

I am sorry Errol's folks are not responding to the Church. I am also a little surprised that Errol doesn't want to talk about the Church or his mission that much. That doesn't sound like the Errol I know, and I'm sure you must be right about how hard he has taken this whole thing. From the sound of things, though, you two seem to be getting along real good. With all of his qualities, which you seem to be very aware of, I might add, he's pretty hard to compete with—especially when I'm nine thousand miles away!

I am excited as well as overwhelmed with my new calling. I will be doing a lot of traveling, and to cover this mission you do TRAVEL! We take in at least half of Australia which, of course, is the size of the United States. We also have New Guinea in our mission, with two sets of missionaries up there. That's one place I would like to go, but President Cook said we probably wouldn't go up there because of our limited travel budget. Another positive thing about this responsibility is getting to know and work with all of the elders in the mission. They really are a great bunch of guys, and almost every one of them seem to want to do well. There are about a half dozen sisters in our mission, and they'll be fun to work with, too. Maybe the best thing about the call is I will still be able to teach potential converts. We have a "mission home" district, and when I'm in town, I get to work with non-members!

Becky, I'm happy! I'm glad I'm here, and I'm thankful for my experiences and the Church and my family and for my friends like Errol and you.

As ever,
Pete

P.S. I don't know when I would be able to get out to my old apartment to get a picture of Mr. Kraft and Mrs. McClaren, but for what it's worth, I've enclosed a picture of me and Elder

Strong. Sorry we aren't wearing colored sweaters so I could identify which one is me!

P.P.S. As you can see, both of the elders in this picture have a full head of hair.

∘———⚓⚓⚓⚓⟩✦

May 8, 1962
Wollstencraft, NSW

Dear Errol,

It's been quite awhile since I heard from you. I hope everything is okay. I hear a little bit about what you are doing from Becky. I just wanted to let you know my new address. This is the mission home, and I have been called to serve as the 2nd C. I don't know what to say about the call except I feel totally inadequate, and I'm going to work my tail off! I will be doing a lot of traveling. In fact, this next week I will be driving up to Brisbane with our mission secretary to hold a conference with President Cook and the Brisbane missionaries. We're driving so we can stop in and visit some of the elders on the way up. That's a 600+ mile drive. President Cook is flying. He's in his late sixties and that much driving may be too strenuous on him. Apparently he has some kind of a heart condition.

I guess you will be starting summer school in less than a month. I suppose Becky is going to be working for her dad, rather than go to school. Right now, I'm not thinking very much about school at all. Too much out here to keep my mind on as you know.

I'd love to hear from you, and I hope you feel that you can talk to me about anything. We've been friends a long time, and I want you to know how much I admire and respect you.

Love,
Pete

∘———⚓⚓⚓⚓⟩✦

May 18, 1962
Tempe, Arizona

Dear Pete,

Congratulations! I'm really proud of you! Just judging from your letters I know your mission president picked the best man to work with him! By the way, in my prayers, I haven't lumped you in with my blessing on ALL the missionaries for awhile now—you actually get your own name mentioned! I'm sure you must have noticed the difference in your performance!

Thank you for your confidence in me and my choices. I don't know whether I'm as sure as you are or not. I'm glad you "hope" they are right. So do I! I'm glad you were "one depressed missionary" when you thought I wasn't going to write anymore. I know *exactly* how you feel.

Am I right—do I detect just a faint bit of jealousy in your last letter? That is flattering, though I can assure you I am not trying to create it! I will admit I am mixed up right now. This choice business has caused me more than a little discomfort. I find myself looking at everything I do and trying to determine what my motive was for doing it and what I really want. That's one thing.

I've also been seeing a lot of Errol and I like him. I'm afraid, quite a bit. Sometimes I worry about him—I don't know whether I should even say this and I want you to promise you won't say anything to anybody—but sometimes I worry about him and the Church. It's not that he's doing anything wrong particularly, it's just that he doesn't appear to want to have that much to do with the Church anymore. He's still working on Sunday, and that doesn't seem to concern him at all. In fact, I don't think he's been out to more than three or four church meetings since coming home. In spite of seeing him this way with the Church, I still like to be with him and that bothers me, too. I mean, I get this feeling that maybe he doesn't feel that strong about the Church anymore and maybe he's moving away from it, and even though I think this is happening, I still want to be around him. I don't know what is happening to me, Pete! Maybe I don't feel as strong about the Church as I thought I did. Could that be? I hope you can understand what I'm trying to say and won't think too bad of me! I wish I could see you and talk to you. I feel good writing to you and getting your letters. You really help me! I mean REALLY help me! I probably shouldn't say this, but I have strong feelings for you, too, and I really feel torn right now.

I'm sorry! I have no business saying anything like that without knowing how you feel and without ever even having seen you. My big mouth's operating out of gear again, and I would rip this letter up and start over again if I hadn't already written so much and it wouldn't take so much time to do it all over! Maybe I want you to know how I'm feeling anyway—I don't know. In any case, it's done, and I'm going to let it stand! You can ignore it, respond to it or stop writing altogether and get me off your back! Speaking of choices—it's yours!

I can tell you are happy! It makes me happy just to read your letters. Thank you!

> *Yours confused,*
> *Becky*

P.S. Thanks loads for the picture! You're both standing so far back I can't even tell which one is you! Neither one in the picture you sent looks like your high school picture at your mother's place! Oh, well, it's nice to know that you at least have a full head of hair!

o—⬤ঁ𝔵

June 1, 1962
Wollstencraft, NSW

Dear Errol,

It's been a couple of months since I heard from you. I hope everything is okay. I have been almost constantly on the road since I last wrote. In fact, this week is the first I've been in the mission home for more than three days in a row since I came into the home! It has been a tremendous experience! I spent a couple of weeks driving up to Brisbane and visiting the elders and holding missionary conferences with President Cook. On the fifth of this month I fly out to a place called Broken Hill. It's a mining town about a thousand miles directly inland from Sydney. I hear it's like the "Old West." I'm looking forward to that.

Becky has kept me pretty well up to date on what's happening with you. It sounds like you two have something going. I have to admit I have some feelings for her, too, but I would never even try to run competition with you, Errol! We're too good of friends for that. Even if I did, I'm afraid I wouldn't be much of a challenge for you! Besides, I've got too much out here to concern myself with without getting "romantically" involved! That's the last thing I need!

I hope everything is going well with you and your life and you are able to maintain the spirit of your mission there at home. I would certainly like to hear from you if you have a minute.

Love,
Pete

o———ooooo⟩⟨

June 1, 1962
Wollstencraft, NSW

Dear Becky,

Thanks for your letter. I didn't get to read it until a couple of days ago. I've been out of town since May 14 and just got back into the mission home day before yesterday. I can tell you I look forward to those letters! That's going to be one disadvantage of traveling—not getting to read my letters right when they come in, but I am REALLY enjoying what I'm doing!

This last few weeks I've been up in Brisbane. It was good to "go back home"! Especially in the winter! Sydney has been a little cool, but not like the town I was in last winter! Brisbane is even warmer than Sydney, so I'm glad I was up there. I even had time to go out to my old area where I served when I first came to Australia. One of the real disappointments of my mission was hearing some months back that this lady, Sister Bloom, who we baptized up there, had fallen away. I visited with her last week. She was nice enough, but the Spirit had gone. She just didn't seem to have any interest in the Church at all. I had had such a tremendous spiritual experience with her and now, at least to her, it appears to have been meaningless.

I've thought a lot about that in the last few days and have come to the conclusion that it wasn't meaningless at all! In fact, it was my spiritual anchor for nearly the first half of my mission! If I hadn't had that experience and the feelings of accomplishment that that brought me, I may not have made it through some of my trials! I can hardly believe what's happened with her, but maybe it just reinforces what you and I have talked about regarding choice. Of course, I don't know what Sister Bloom's ultimate choice will be, but she certainly had a lot more knowledge about the truthfulness of the Church when she made this choice to be inactive than she did before. I won't give up on her, though, and I am going to continue to write to her.

135

Speaking of free agency and choice, I appreciate your concerns about Errol. Maybe this is just his "difficult" time, just like I had eight to ten months ago. I think he must be struggling to find himself. I've known Errol all my life, and if there was anyone I'd bet on choosing the right way, it's Errol! You should have read some of the letters he wrote me about his testimony! He's been as close to me as any brother, and I'd literally stake my life on him.

It sounds like you're going through the same kind of struggle. I believe I know you well enough through your letters to "stake my life" on you, too. You guys better not let me down, or I'm dead! Seriously, I don't think you ever have to worry about what your choices are going to be! I appreciate your openness about your feelings, and I'm flattered that you would "admit" to liking me. Flattered is probably not as appropriate a word as OVERWHELMED! I'm afraid I'm no competition to Errol, though. He's got it all, just like you say, and I'm just now discovering all that I don't have. Hopefully I've started to do something about it! I've got a long way! I don't blame you for feeling the way you do about him. I would think something was wrong with you if you didn't!

I guess what I'm trying to say is he's there, and I'm here. You know him. The only thing you know about me is my letters. If we were both there together, I don't think you would even have the slightest doubt about "concentrating" on Errol! Please don't get me wrong—I know if I let myself, I could really like you! In fact, to be honest, I already do. A lot! (I guess this is "mutual confessions"!) But I don't feel it's fair to you or Errol to let my "ghost" complicate your relationship. I mean, you've never seen me, and you've never even heard my voice! All you know of me is my letters and what my mother says—remember, "take it with a grain of salt!" Please don't think I'm just trying to be a martyr or something. I just want everybody to be happy.

There's another thing, too. What I am doing out here is the most important thing in the world to me right now, and I don't want anything to take away from my effectiveness. If you knew me, you would know how much I already have to struggle with myself to concentrate on what I'm supposed to be doing and to try to keep in tune. If I was always worrying about what you and Errol were doing or what you were thinking about me or whether or not you'd be there when I got home, which I would do if our relationship was anything more than "friends" right now, I think it would ruin the last part of my mission!

I hope you understand what I'm trying to say. You scare me, Becky! I've never felt this way about anybody before, and I'm not going to let it go any further—not right now anyway. When I get home and if you're still there and if you and Errol for whatever reason decided things wouldn't work out between you and the shock of seeing what I'm really like isn't too great for you, I'd like to get to know you a lot better! But for the next four or five months I'd like us to be friends—really good friends—and I'd like to be able to write to you like I have been and I'd like to get your letters back. I hope you understand what I'm trying to say and that you won't be offended by it. I just think it would be the best way to do it—for everybody!

Well, I didn't mean to write so much about all that. This is already a long letter, and I haven't told you about my Brisbane trip at all. It's late now—nearly midnight—and I've got to get up at 5:30 in the morning so I'll close this "first chapter" and write "Chapter Two" tomorrow. Don't worry, you don't have to write me two letters in answer!

> *As ever,*
> *Pete*

P.S. I haven't heard from Errol for a couple of months. Tell him he OWES me!

o—∞∞∞⊃r

Dear Becky,

Well, as you can see I didn't get the rest of that letter written the next day. I have been so busy it seems like I just get out of bed to get back in! I have been working with the elders throughout the Sydney area, teaching them how to do street surveys. These surveys are really effective, but it takes a little "courage" to do. We stand on the sidewalk in a busy area of town and stop people as they come by and say something like, "Hello, I'm taking a survey and if you have a minute, I'd like to ask you a couple of questions. I'm American as you probably can tell, and I've come over from the United States to tell people about the Mormon Church. Have you ever heard of the Mormon Church? Do you know very much about it? My companion and I would like to come over in an evening and take 30 minutes to tell you a little more about it. Would next Wednesday at 7:00 p.m. be okay?"

That's all there is to it, and boy does it work well! Working with a set of elders, we can book them solid with night time meetings for two weeks in a row just spending about an hour surveying. Anyway, that's why I haven't written the second part of my letter until now.

At this moment I'm about 15,000 feet in the air, flying to Broken Hill. It's about 1000 miles inland from Sydney and is out in the middle of nowhere! At least that's what I've been told, and that's the way it looks. I keep looking down to see a town or something, but there's nothing! Miles and miles of nothing! This plane I'm on is a two engine job, and the way it keeps jerking around it feels like a jeep on a rutty, dirt road! I hope I don't need it, but I'm glad I've got a "little bag" in the pocket of the seat in front of me!

We've had one stop so far, but I don't think there will be anymore until we get to Broken Hill. When we were stopping,

I could feel the plane slow down like it was getting ready to come in for a landing, and I looked out to see where we were. We were nowhere! There was no town, and there was no airport! All there was was a dirt runway down below with a fence around it to keep the cows off it, and there were two outhouses sitting at the side of the landing strip. There was a car parked at the fence and a couple of people with luggage standing there waiting. That was it! The pilot doesn't stop unless he sees somebody down their waiting! We picked up the people, they paid the stewardess for the ticket and sat down. It was just like a bus stopping at a corner!

I'm anxious to see Broken Hill!

Well, the real purpose of this letter was to tell you about my trip to Brisbane a couple of weeks ago. The mission secretary and I drove the mission president's car up. It's a big Ford Fairlane and cost about as much as a Cadillac in the U.S. would cost because it has to be built special here.

Driving up there was quite a deal! The road is narrow and just two lanes, and you see little pieces of glass all down the side of the road where windshields (they call them "wind-screens") have broken from rocks kicked up by passing cars! We saw a lot of kangaroos, too—they're all over the place!

The country was beautiful—rolling hills of lush green and hillsides checkered with sugar cane fields. It was fun traveling, and everywhere we stopped we would try to ask the "Golden Questions."

It was kind of funny the reaction we got from this petrol (gas) station attendant. He was about our age, and when he found out we were Americans, he started asking us some questions about why we were over here. We told him a little bit about the Church and while I reached in my pocket to pay him, I said, "We are over here on our own time and expense preaching the gospel because we know it's true, and we are willing to make these kinds of sacrifices because we do know it's true.

He looked up at me out of the corner of his eye, then looked over at our big Ford Fairlane and then at our clothes (we were both wearing suits and NOBODY our age has a suit in Australia!) and then he looked down as I peeled off a twenty pound note from the wad of bills the mission president had given me to pay for two weeks worth of motels and traveling expenses! He looked back up at me, cocked his head and said, "Mate, that's my kind of sacrifice!" He took the note and gave me change. All my companion and I could do was laugh and try to explain. He obviously didn't believe us, but said "Yes" when we asked if we could send some missionaries to see him. I think maybe he was thinking if the Church did this for us, just think what it would do for him!

The rest of the trip up was uneventful, and I spent my time in Brisbane holding conferences with President Cook and the Brisbane missionaries and visiting with the elders to show them how to do the street surveys. We had a fantastic experience! Elder Brighton (one of the Brisbane elders) was standing on a corner trying to pick out someone to interview. We only choose men from late teenage to about age 40 because girls and women think we're trying to pick them up, and the older men want nothing to do with us!

Anyway, while he was standing there, this man about 70 years old tapped him on the shoulder and asked him for directions. Elder Brighton gave him directions and then was going to turn away from him because he was too old to interview, but he was prompted to interview him anyway. When the old man found out Elder Brighton was a Mormon missionary, tears started to come down his face, and he told Elder Brighton that he had heard the gospel in New Zealand about a year ago and had read the Book of Mormon but just couldn't make the decision to be baptized.

He said his life was in total chaos right now and that that morning he had pleaded with his Heavenly Father to lead him and show him some sign as to what he was supposed to do with his life. Then he looked at Elder Brighton and said, "Meeting you is the sign! Will you please baptize me?"

We went straight to the chapel, filled up the font and baptized him. His face reminded me of Sister Bloom's when she was baptized. It was glowing! It was a mighty experience!

By the way, I forgot to thank you in the "first chapter" of this letter I mailed the other day for you singling me out from ALL of the other missionaries in your prayers! As I said before, I need all the help I can get!

> *As ever,*
> *Pete*

P.S. I've been thinking a lot about what I said in "Chapter One." I hope you take it right. I mean, I hope you don't think I'm not interested in you or don't want you to be interested in me—it's just the opposite and given the circumstances and all, that's the problem! I am and I do and I can't do anything about it! Most of all I don't want to do anything to hurt either you or Errol.

o—꜀꜀꜀꜀ꝏ꜀꜀Ӿ

> June 10, 1962
> Tempe, Arizona

Dear Pete,

You seem to "give up" pretty easy! I mean, from the sound of your letter (at least "part one"—I haven't gotten "part two" yet, if you ever sent it, and I've been purposely waiting to get "part two" before writing this, but since I haven't gotten "part two" and don't know whether I'll ever get it, I'm going to write this anyway!). I don't think you are really that interested in whether I'm around or not when you get home ("mutual confessions" or not)! It sounds like you are more concerned with being "bothered" by me while you're on your mission and maybe even concerned that you might have some sort of obligation to me when you come home! If that's the case, maybe we'd just better stop the letter writing all together so you can concentrate on your mission, and I won't be a BIG distraction!

I knew I shouldn't have sent my last letter, and as soon as I dropped it into the mailbox, I wished I could have gotten it back. Well, anyway, whatever I said then doesn't apply now— at least as far as my feelings for you are concerned! You said you would like us to just be friends for the next four or five months, "really good friends." I've got a better idea—let's just be friends, not "really good" or anything, and let's not put a time limit on it!

Sincerely,
Becky

o———ᴄᴍᴍᴏ)ʞ

June 11, 1962
Tempe, Arizona

Dear Pete,

I just got "Chapter Two"—please ignore what I said in response to "Chapter One"! I wasn't going to mail that either, but I did! It's "Hoof and Mouth" again, and I'm asking you for an opportunity to pull the hoof back out! If it's all right with you, could we go back to the way we were before I wrote that letter and before you read it? I DO understand what you're saying, and I just got my ego in the way. You're right—as usual. I am more confused then ever! Sometimes I wish Daddy never took this job at ASU, and we still lived up in Utah. Then none of this would have ever happened!

I've decided not to say anything more about Errol and me or about you and me. Que sera, sera. I love your letters, and I hope they continue. As long as they do, so will mine!

By the way, I'd be careful if I were you about laying your life on the line about somebody else's choices. It seems to me

142

that that kind of a bet ought to be made only if you have total control of the outcome! Heaven knows, I hope you're right, though—for both mine and Errol's sakes!

I really envy your traveling! I've been on a plane once, and that was a small one when Dad paid a pilot to take him and me up over Salt Lake City for my twelfth birthday. I've been up to Yellowstone Park and over to Las Vegas, and that's about the extent of my travel. Your flying trip sounded fascinating—outhouses and all—and I'm looking forward to hearing about "Broken Hill!" Your Brisbane trip sounded interesting, too—especially that "sacrifice" line to the gas station attendant! I mean really, Pete, living in mansions, eating five meals a day, driving fancy cars around and all is pretty tough to take! I hope you can survive it all!

Well, I'm going to get this in the mail so you'll get it within a day or two (or even the same day if I'm lucky!) of my other letter. Just for the record's sake, you don't have to send me two letters in response—we're ignoring my first one, remember!

> *As always,*
> *Becky*

P.S. I really am sorry about that first letter!

o—aaaa×

> June 15, 1962
> Mesa, Arizona

Dear Pete,

I haven't written earlier because I've been pretty busy. I'm working about 25 hours a week and then I've been seeing Becky nearly every day, too, so I'm lucky just to get some studying in, let alone write a letter. I'm glad to be back in school. I like associating with non-LDS. The people in the

Church get so wrapped up with meetings and positions and their own righteousness that they don't even know there is another world going on out here.

My bishop (here in Mesa) has been trying to get me to go in to see him, but I've been too busy. Besides, I really don't have anything to talk to him about. His counselor called on me the other day and asked me to teach a Sunday School class, but I told him that I did more than my share for the last year and a half, and it was time for a good, long rest! I wish they would stop bugging me.

Things are getting thick between Becky and me. Don't be surprised if you get a little announcement in the next month or so! Well, I've got to get going.

Errol

P.S. Congratulations on being made 2nd C.—I guess.

o—∞∞∞⟩r

June 23, 1962
Wollstencraft, NSW

Dear Becky,

I just got back in town! After we flew back from Broken Hill, the mission secretary and I left the next day and toured New South Wales by car—visiting all of the missionaries in the outlying areas outside of Sydney. That was a l-o-n-g trip! We put just over 2300 miles on the car. I was glad your letter was here waiting for me. I was really kind of worried after I sent my "Chapter One" letter that I hadn't made myself very clear. Anyway, I got your letter, and it made me feel a lot better! Apparently the letter I got was your second letter, and I never received that first one. From what you said in your second one, I'm really curious what you said in your first one! You must have really let me have it or something.

144

I also got a letter from Errol—finally! I'm not sure I wanted that one. I don't think I know him anymore. It was very short, and he implied that you two are practically engaged. If that's the case, I wish you the best! I mean that!

I had a great trip to Broken Hill! What a place! It's like a town in the "Old West"! It's windy and dirty and the buildings are mostly made of wood and tin. Most of the men there work in the mines and are a rough and tumble lot. The Church has a branch there, and they have just built a chapel, too. There have been a lot of baptisms in the last few years, and I think there's something like a hundred to a hundred and fifty members.

Broken Hill is really isolated from everything. It sits all by itself out in the outback and the closest town I think is about two hundred miles of dirt road away! The members are really friendly, though, and there is a pretty high activity rate there. I stayed over Sunday and visited church.

My flight back to Sydney wasn't anywhere near as rough as my flight out. I was only back in the mission home for one night before we took off on our New South Wales "tour." Basically, we were teaching the elders how to do "street surveys" and visiting the branches and branch presidencies to "pep" them up!

I'm tired! But I love what I'm doing! I love these people, Becky, and I just feel like I should be going day and night to help them! I'm practically doing that with all this travel! In a week I'm going to be on the road again! This time I will be flying up to Queensland. I'll stop in Brisbane again and then fly up the coast to Rockhampton, Townsville and all the way up to Cairns (look on your map—it's at the "top" of Australia!). That's going to be about a four or five thousand mile round trip, and I'm going to be gone the better part of a month, so I won't get any letters written to you until the end of July—or be able to receive any letters until then! Oh, well, I'm busy enough that hopefully I can keep my mind off those letters!

Again, thanks for letting me write to you, and I hope

things work out for you and Errol. Please don't worry about me in all this. I understand.

Sincerely,
Pete

P.S. I'm really curious what you put in that first letter!

o——☞

June 25, 1962
Wollstencraft, NSW

Dear Errol,

Thanks for your letter. I was beginning to think you had broken your writing hand or something! I've been pretty busy myself. I have been traveling all over the mission and am going to be leaving by plane for parts north! I'll fly all the way up to Cairns, about 2000 miles away from here! I enjoy the flying and the traveling, and I enjoy meeting the people and the missionaries! I even get to do some proselyting when I'm in town. Right now we've just started working with this sixteen-year-old young man who lives in the ghettos in Sydney. The other elders in the "home" here will teach him while I'm on this trip. I won't get back until the latter part of July!

I've been debating whether or not to say anything about what I'm thinking, but I've decided I'm going to. I hope you understand what I'm trying to say here and know that I'm saying it because I love you. I don't know what's going on with your life right now, Errol, but from the way your letters sound and all, the Church doesn't seem to be all that important to you. That's a little hard for me to understand. After all the things we've done together and the fantastic mission you served I thought I knew you, and I really don't understand why you're doing what you seem to be doing (or not doing!).

146

You know this Church is true as well as I do! I'm beginning to realize that knowing it's true isn't anywhere near as important as wanting to live it! It's this choice business again!

Do you remember the struggle I had about my choices just before Dad died. I didn't really know it at the time, but I was struggling with myself to determine just who I was and what I wanted to be. Is that where you are now, Errol? I really thought I knew you, Errol! I just can't believe all the good works you've done and all the talks we've had were just a facade! I know you know about choice! Are you making choices now you really want to make? I mean, do you really want to drift away from the Church and become "non-involved"?

Listen brother, Becky is probably the neatest girl I've ever known and you owe it to her to shape up and get your act together so you can really make her happy! I know for a fact she is worried about you, and if you keep on doing what you're doing, you're really going to blow it with her!

I hope you know I'm saying all this because you're my best friend and I love you!

Love,
Pete

o———————⅜

July 15, 1962
Tempe, Arizona

Dear Pete,

I think this will be my last letter—at least for awhile. I am horribly confused right now. Errol has asked me not to write anymore. Given our present involvement, I can see his point and I guess I agree.

This is the most painful experience of my life!

Becky

147

P.S. No matter what happens between Errol and me, I want you to know that you have touched my life.

—⚬—◦◦◦◦◦◦—◦—

July 26, 1962
Wollstencraft, NSW

Dear Becky,

When I got back from my trip up north, I found both of your letters here—that "first" letter of yours that was lost in the mail and this last one.

I told you before that nearly a year ago I had come to some conclusions about myself. It took my dad's death to finally make me willing to pull back the curtains to see who I was. As I looked, I saw all of my inadequacies and weaknesses glaring at me like some giant neon sign. But I also saw someone who wanted to be like Jesus Christ, and I knew from that moment on my direction was set.

The other day in Cairns, I had an experience that verified that choice. It was the most sacred experience of my life. Cairns is very tropical and is surrounded by jungle. The humidity is so high and the temperature so hot (even now in the middle of winter!) that the elders never wear ties or coats, and their clothes mildew if they leave them hanging in the closet for longer than a couple of days without taking them out in the sun to air!

We did our regular "stuff"—met with the branch leaders, conducted street surveys, etc. Then our last day there the elders took us to meet an aborigine family they were working with. The family lived out at the edge of town in an "Abo" settlement. There were no houses—just corrugated tin roofs perched on top of randomly shaped wooden poles. There were blankets strung up dividing the living space into "rooms." The only running water was an old hand pump in the center of the camp. Cooking was done over an open fire and what few pots, pans or "furniture" there was looked like it had been rescued from a garbage dump! The people were all dirty (how could they bathe?) and what clothes they had on were virtually rags.

At first I didn't dare touch them. They were almost repulsive! But as I looked at them, I could see that they were my brothers and sisters, and I felt this almost indescribable love for them. I wanted to hold the little children and kiss them, and I wanted to put my arms around the older ones and kiss them. I wanted to tell them about Jesus Christ, and I wanted them to know what I knew—that they were sons and daughters of God and Jesus Christ was their brother and they could become like Him.

I stood there looking at these beautiful, dark, dusty faces framed with tangled, matted hair, and I forgot the smell and the dirt and all I could see was their eyes and I felt like I was looking right inside them, and they were looking inside me and they could see what I felt, and they could understand what I wanted to tell them. Then we all started to cry, and I felt my arms reach out, and these little kids came over and grabbed hold of my knees and I reached down and picked them up one at a time and kissed them and hugged them. Then I hugged their parents and kissed them, too. I didn't say a word. Nobody said a word—not the other elders, not anybody. Finally we left. I couldn't stop crying for a long time.

For a few minutes I actually felt the kind of love for those people that I think Christ feels for me. I want more than anything for that feeling to be with me always.

Judging from the spirit of his last letter, Errol seems to have made a choice, too. It appears to be your turn now, Becky. Or have you already made it? For what it's worth, I know you are a stunningly beautiful girl, no matter what color of sweater you wear.

Love,
Pete

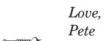

149

August 4, 1962
Mesa, Arizona

Pete—

I don't know what you said in your last letter to Becky, but she is all upset. My guess is you preached to her like you did to me. You're coming off more than just a little self-righteous here, don't you think? What I do with my life and what Becky does with her life are our business! I really think your mission has warped your sense of judgment!

In any case, I *insist* you not write Becky anymore and as she has already told you, she's not writing to you either.

I asked her to marry me about three weeks ago, and we are planning an October wedding. You can consider this our official announcement.

Errol

P.S. You don't need to respond to this letter. In fact, I think it best that we just let the letter writing drop and when you get back, maybe we'll bump into each other at ASU.

o———⊸⊸⊸⟩⊀

October 10, 1962
Tempe, Arizona

Dear Pete,

I know it's been three months since I last wrote, but in case you are still interested after all this time, it *was* time for my choice. I'd like a chance to talk to you about it in person if it's all right with you. Your mother has invited me to go with her and your family to the airport to meet you on the 23rd. I'll be the one in the red sweater!

Love,
Becky

P.S. You can call me Enid if you want. I'm beginning to like that name, too.

o———ᴐᴍᴍᴐ⋊